# THE TRADE

A Savio Mendes Novella

Lesann Berry

Isinglass Press
SILVERLAKE, WASHINGTON

Isinglass Press
P.O. Box 1731
Castle Rock, Washington 98611
www.isinglasspress.com

Publisher's Note: This is a work of fiction. Names, characters, places, and incidents are a product of the author's imagination. Locales and public names are sometimes used for atmospheric purposes. Any resemblance to actual people, living or dead, or to businesses, companies, events, institutions, or locales is completely coincidental.

Cover Design by www.cheekycovers.com
Interior Design by www.BookDesignTemplates.com

Ordering Information:
Quantity sales. Special discounts are available on quantity purchases by corporations, associations, and others. For details, contact the "Special Sales Department" at the address above.

The Trade / Lesann Berry. -- 1st ed.
ISBN 978-1-939316-10-3

*To those who blur the lines and walk the edge.*

*A man is known by the company he avoids.*
– ANONYMOUS

# CHAPTER ONE

SAVIO MENDES HUNCHED over his desk, a fist pressed against his growling stomach. Nothing sounded appetizing. His inability to make a simple choice about what to eat for lunch was symptomatic of larger issues. The phone on his desk rang. The shrill buzz of noise threw him back in time and he froze. Immobile in his chair, mind riveted on the flash of light that burst in his memory, his esophagus closed up and threatened to shut down his breathing. Panic bloomed. He clutched the edge of his desk, the metal tepid under his fingers.

The air conditioner kicked on. An artificial breeze cooled the tiny dots of sweat on his forehead and after a few seconds the temporary paralysis drained away. He swiped at the moisture and glared at his palm. The telltale slick deepened his scowl. He hated these sudden flashbacks and how they increased in frequency the more sedentary he became. Maybe he should skip lunch and go running instead, boost some endorphins into seducing his mind everything was okay. The air outside the building might be oppressive with heat but inside the temperature range was locked into a constant seventy degrees. He figured the sterile warm environment must be a company policy. Every thermostat was housed inside a tamper-proof lock box, each one mounted to the wall so no employee could raise or lower the ambient comfort zone.

So here he sat, sweating again, for no reason.

He straightened and scrubbed his palms across his denim-clad thighs. Fridays were dress-down days at the office and he never missed the opportunity to lower company standards by ditching more formal attire. Today he'd pulled on his standard casual uniform of jeans, a black t-shirt, and nondescript black boots. With black hair and blue eyes that matched his fashion choices, Marjorie, the office assistant assigned to his floor, always offered a flirty quip about his appearance as he stepped off the elevator.

"You're so monochromatic on Fridays, Mr. Mendes."

He never knew how to respond. He guessed the silly woman didn't understand the meaning of the word but for all he knew she might hold an advanced degree in art theory and be cognizant that black was not a color. In that case, then technically, he supposed she might be correct. As always, he ignored her inviting smiles, grunted out a terse morning greeting and disappeared into his office. Once there, he squatted behind his desk, counting the hours until a new case landed on his schedule. The waiting period between field assignments was tortuous for him.

He shook his head and tried to clear his mind of irrelevant details. His thoughts wandered off track, another symptom the psych doctors warned him about. Every soldier knew the risks and signs of post-traumatic stress disorder. Anyone who stayed in the service, especially those who saw enough active duty, dealt with the affliction sooner or later. He'd just decided later was better for him. Except the PTSD wasn't patient. The general malaise which eroded his peace of mind continued to grow.

The interruption of his sleep patterns had not abated. Most nights he was lucky if he managed more than two hours of undisturbed sleep at a stretch. He'd still get his rest but doing so required an accumulation of hours. The future outlook, if not his actual prognosis, was grim.

Even his recent two week training exercise in the jungle failed to improve his situation. At one time that sort of activity would have offered a welcome excuse to run amok and shoot guns. Now those kinds of activities left him unmoved. Being assigned to play nursemaid to new recruits just emphasized how much his physical prowess and endurance had waned. The task grated on his nerves even more since his return to Los Angeles and the realization he'd been reduced to a personnel trainer had struck. At thirty-five he felt like an old man.

He checked an instinctive response to knead the line of scar tissue at the juncture of his hip and thigh. Instead, he swiveled his gaze to the single window. His compact office featured only one view but he appreciated the glimpse of blue sky. Masked on all sides by off-white clouds, the promise of a reprieve from the heat which had blanketed the Los Angeles basin all week looked dim. Rain eluded the forecasters. California faced another year of too few spring showers and a summer filled with raging wildfires.

His belly gurgled. Hamstrung by indecision, his inability to even choose a restaurant for lunch, provoked speculation about how long it would take before depression or PTSD symptoms impacted his ability to do his job. Professional ethics be damned, he needed to work.

Hunger growled again. Shouldn't he want *something?*

Today was no different than any other, he told himself. That wasn't a complete lie. Just before sunrise he'd wakened with the now-familiar sense of fatalism choking in his throat. After a long slow slide to rock bottom, he sensed his end approaching. Without melodrama, he pictured an image of his termination date, an indeterminate month and day flickering on the horizon. Despite what he'd survived, and all the struggles he'd endured to come back from the damage to his body, thoughts of dying no longer alarmed him.

Maybe it was time.

He desired nothing. Other than meeting nutritional demands, food held little allure. Sex offered even less. He couldn't work up the initiative to seduce a woman. He preferred the pleasure-without-strings value of one-night stands when he conducted a relationship with the female half of the species. But he disliked easy pickings. Neither did he utilize the unfortunates who plied their bodies at the local bar scene. Even the runway model he'd escorted around town last winter had droned on about their future until the chatter stunted his interest.

Sex involved too much effort.

Just like lunch.

His stomach cramped. *Fuck.* He had to eat before gastric acid melted a hole through his belly. He pushed up from his desk and a shift in the light indicated someone stood in the doorway. He raised his eyes and found Henri pushing the door shut. *Fuck.* He didn't want another one of Henri's pep talks about how grateful he should feel to have this job.

Henri waved him back to his chair and his flash of annoyance was shouldered aside by resentment.

Savio stood. "I'm just off to lunch, Henri. Can I bring you some food on my way back?"

"Sit, my boy." Henri Cavalleri brandished a thick folder in one hand. He crossed the carpeted floor and tossed the dossier onto the desk. The document slid to a halt in front of Savio's chair. "I've got an assignment for you. How does a stint in Mexico City sound? This is a slick offer, not like your usual task."

Locked in his office for less than a week, Savio was already climbing the walls. Any job that promised a reprieve from staring at the cracks in the ceiling was worth considering. Savio remained on his feet just to be contrary as Henri strode back and forth. Curious, he rotated the file and flipped open the cover. The name Eduardo Almeida was typed on the first page. He scanned the text, another drug cartel.

*Interesting.*

"I want you in Mexico for surveillance. You hang around the neighborhood, watch the comings and goings, and get to know the people next door. The set-up is superb."

The agency produced and updated field summaries about key players. Almeida's name brought back details. If his recall proved accurate, Almeida was the poster boy for success among certain circles. The man had scrabbled up from a poverty-stricken childhood to establish and operate a multinational business. It was his product of choice that upset most people. He exported methamphetamine. As the C.E.O. of an up-and-coming cartel industry, Almeida's efforts to wrestle control of a significant portion of meth traffic north of the border had succeeded. The ruthless administration of violence marked his trail.

"Last year, the Treasury Department held the Almeida organization responsible for as much as twenty percent of the methamphetamine imported into the United States from Mexico." Henri said.

"That's a lot of product."

"Almeida heads a drug consortium that until eighteen months ago was unremarkable."

Savio nodded to indicate he was listening. He'd read a preliminary review of this man. With aspirations of grandeur, Almeida had enlarged his operation with systematic precision. One of his favorite pastimes appeared to be grinding smaller pushers and distributors under his heel. The coup which pushed him into the spotlight involved the vicious overthrow of the long-established Hermosa drug network.

In the tradition of political violence around the world and throughout history, entire families had disappeared over night. Almeida's operatives moved in and seized control. Evidence of the bloody altercation had featured in the headlines on the international news channels every evening for weeks. He recalled the lurid headlines: headless corpses discovered in mineshafts, busloads of tourists gunned down at intersections, and a garrison of corrupt local police executed. No one was safe.

What didn't translate to the outer world was how drugs represented a way of life to these people. These events were just part of the day-to-day activity of survival. This was the business of *La Familia*.

In the same manner some families produced cops or plumbers or lawyers, cartels spit out successive generations of offspring who planned to fill daddy's shoes. Filial expectations pushed the young into the trade and the cycle of organized crime continued. Italy birthed the *Cosa Nostra*, the Americas delivered cartels.

The word for that, Savio thought back to his childhood in Brazil, was tradition.

"Local government officials turn a blind eye to the internal conflict. They're happy to let the pushers fight among themselves."

Savio turned the page. Henri was over-simplifying. He'd left out the part about law enforcement discovering they were ill-prepared to respond to subsequent waves of violence. The good guys floundered and lost ground.

Surveillance sucked but Mexico City offered a food paradise. Since his stomach was determined to interfere with the rest of his life, the offer held the promise of personal satisfaction too.

Savio liked action. He preferred the jungle, more at home with dirt and grit than a nice clean house in a fancy neighborhood. He moved like a ghost in the shadows, no more than an echo down a hallway. He blended into natural settings better than city landscapes. Despite that, he could appreciate Henri's rapture over an old man's version of undercover work. It almost sounded like a vacation.

"If we cut Almeida's organization off at the knees, it raises our position in the international community. This task could open opportunities in other parts of the world."

Savio flipped another page and scanned the synopsis. He suspected Mexico City representatives contracted the company to clean up the mess. Seeking external assistance to curtail the activities of the Almeida organization was smart. Let the outsiders do the dirty work. Provide the frightened and insecure public with a solution and a potential scapegoat—it's what he would do.

Interest piqued and appetite stimulated in anticipation of traditional Mexican cuisine, he closed the cover on the file and sat down in his chair.

Henri continued. "We've leased a cover house in a perfect neighborhood. It's located outside the main boroughs of the city but is filled with residents involved in various fingers of the industry. You'll fit right in."

Savio thought Almeida must have passed the up-and-comer status if he was under this level of investigation. Despite his lethargy, curiosity sparked. His maternal grandparents emigrated to the U.S. from the capital of Mexico. He liked the city, enjoyed the contrast of ancient next to modern. He was seized by the desire to explore temples raised to ancestral gods where they squatted beside present-day shrines dedicated to finance.

And, Mexico offered a welcome reprieve from the endless monotony of his desk. This was the life he'd desired, might as well embrace the bad with the good. Besides, he wanted Henri out of his office. "When do I leave?"

"No more than a week."

A man of spare proportions, Henri paced the narrow strip of carpet in his typical restless fashion. His path followed a precise trajectory between the couch and the desk. The visual produced another flashback for Savio. Years before, the enlisted men had called Henri the terrier. The description, still apt, fit the way the man worried and tore at a problem until the issue was resolved or dismembered.

Now Henri halted and stared down at him, his dark eyes intense and focused. "I'm offering you a prime opportunity to demonstrate your move upstairs was a strategic decision."

The words grated. Savio had proved his worth. He'd shown initiative and perseverance since his first day on the job. As a result, his promotion through the internal ranks accelerated and he climbed ahead of other employees who'd been on the payroll longer. The back-handed compliment to Henri's successful recruitment did a lot to improve both their standing in the company. Henri might have introduced Savio to James Cole, the head honcho, but he'd earned his ascent in the hierarchy.

Savio's concentration wandered as Henri talked. He fingered the dossier on his desktop. When the narcotics trade was your industry, you identified big players as readily as day traders knew stock. Even so, he wearied of hearing the same rhetoric.

Henri's pep talk ran out of steam. He switched gears and pulled up a chair, leaning back and waiting.

Savio quirked a brow. "Tell me the rest."

"You've been in the field for a long time, maybe too long, but I want you to do more than just observe on this operation. Between you and me, we need real inside intel from this job."

*Another intriguing development.*

This wasn't the first time Henri had wanted to enlarge the scope of an operative's field task. In the military Henri directed Savio's team to work on behalf of the government. Now they fulfilled a similar function except the pay was better and the clients more varied.

"What am I looking for?" Savio spoke in Portuguese, their shared first language.

Henri answered in the same. "Get involved. Make yourself indispensable. Our client wants to know how to dissolve this organization."

Savio sneered. Then words erupted from his mouth. "It is not possible to shut down a cartel, Henri. You know this. The organizations are like snakes, shedding their skin and taking on new identities. The organism never expires."

Henri shrugged. "My orders come from upstairs."

"As the last line of defense between the public and orga-nized production, companies such as our employer offer a spe-cialized and ultra-violent service." Savio spoke the words in a dull voice. The party line was a bit more polished for public consumption but the gist was the same. "We know drug cartels are sophisticated operations. An essential part of today's global economy, they're sanctioned by officials and funded through corporations."

"Men like you and me, we follow orders, Savio."

Nothing much had changed. He studied the dossier, flipping through the remaining pages. In truth, cartels exemplified successful and profitable international trade which explained why their reach extended into every country on earth. Savio focused on eradication and he was good at his job but the scope and breadth of any single organization made it impossible to destroy – much less the network of interrelated relationships that crisscrossed the globe.

"I'll do it." He told Henri without even looking up. He closed the file and spun the folder on his desk, plans already taking shape in his head.

Henri outlined details with military precision and Savio's attention went sideways again. A decorated war hero, Henri had disappeared from the limelight overnight. Years had passed before Savio saw him again. He'd offered employment. Savio accepted and now they worked together, sort of. Savio held the frontline, ducking bullets and avoiding traps rigged with razor wire. Henri controlled direction, manipulating scenery and offering up dossiers. Of late, the jobs followed a progression of violence and increased risk that climbed in an arc straight up the company slope.

Savio skyrocketed to the top of the food chain.

Henri expected thanks for the opportunity but Savio knew his success had more to do with his not-so-dormant death wish. At the end of every mission waited an empty hole of blackness which threatened to engulf him. The cold ache that never loosened its talons on his right leg served as a stark reminder of mortality. Some days embracing the maw of nothingness offered a certain appeal.

Little tied him to this world. With no great inclination to survive, the other operatives considered him a dangerous and unwanted partner. Okay with him. He preferred to work alone. On really bad days he saw himself as broken, a fractured soul, a soldier who'd died along the road and failed to fall down.

Henri was staring at him.

He'd wandered again.

"I said your official role is to gather intelligence about Almeida's operation. Pay special attention to finding detailed specifications on distribution routes."

This meant his unofficial goal was to infiltrate the circle of confederates as high up in the cartel as he could reach, sans the standard provisos of no bullets, knives, or torture. Savio didn't hold out much hope. The power structure of family-run networks was traditionally comprised of clusters of related members. Outsiders were not invited in.

Henri stood up. "You know the rhetoric about following company rules."

Savio gave a curt nod. Personnel were instructed to adhere to all official guidelines while in the public eye. Not so different than military edicts in that regard. "Got it memorized. Do not kill anyone who does not need killing. Do not leave witnesses. If you find it necessary to leave a witness, make them an accomplice."

"Excellent."

Savio thought he detected a note of disdain in the word. In the jungles, Savio's ability to slip undetected through the greenery earned him the code name of spirit, a reputation unknown to his American colleagues. Or at least it had been until one night the previous December, when Henri got chatty over drinks with a couple of new trainees and over-shared. Reliving the glory years, he'd told stories about Savio and some of their special missions. His team had received medals and commendations for their success, for what that meant. But ever since that evening, the office staff treated him with careful deference. Savio recognized fear in their discomfort.

Another reason to get back into the field as quick as possible.

His years in the army were long past and the jolt of adrenalin he'd enjoyed before the beginning of any new mission was a dim memory but as he contemplated the file on his desk, a sense of expectation began to raise his spirits.

The bloody retaliation between Mexican cartels had escalated to such a fever pitch that government officials outsourced for an intervention. That's where he and Henri entered the scene, collecting intelligence and determining how to take things apart. The narcotics trade had gone international. Few countries didn't benefit in some way from the import or export of designer drugs across their borders.

Everybody knew the good fight was a losing battle.

In his twenty-two months with the firm, he'd participated in a wider variety of tasks than his previous five years in private security. His current employment offered work that more closely resembled his time in military service. Just like his days as a soldier, his relationship with upper management grew in direct relation to his successful completion of each job. That success also reflected well on Henri. Jobs and tasks were handpicked for his special skill-set. Savio suspected the company principals remained clueless about the savage nature of his army past but maybe they didn't care. One did not become the successful CEO of a paid military corporation without testicles carved from granite.

"This job is different in several important ways. First, it's an undercover role. The identification you choose is up to you."

After his mother's death, Savio had disconnected from filial relationships. Now he used his own name and enjoyed the touch of brazenness.

"The intel we have on Almeida indicates a man capable of extremes. There is an unsubstantiated report of him personally executing a competitor and then hurrying home for his nephew's fifth birthday party."

This news did not surprise Savio. He'd known men without conscience. He'd killed some of them. Of late, he'd begun to worry how much his stripes differed from theirs.

"We know Almeida has a strong presence in Mexico City. The cartel actively seeks to expand holdings to the north." Henri leaned over and slapped his hand on the top of the desk. "We stop it now or we'll battle the same drugs on the streets of L.A."

Savio didn't rise to that bit of hyperbole. Henri didn't give a rat's ass about his adopted city. Right now, Savio didn't either. The job offered opportunity and a fat paycheck. For the moment, that was enough. Savio's current trajectory aimed in a downward spiral, his velocity increasing at a measured rate. By the time he hit rock bottom, he figured the impact should leave an impressive crater. His only pleasure these days was outmaneuvering the gnarled hand of fate. One day the old crone would catch his shirt collar in a firm grip and shake his bones. Until then he might as well play with fire.

"Excellent, Henri. When do I leave?"

# CHAPTER TWO

TEN DAYS LATER Savio exited the terminal of Benito Juarez International Airport. The evening air was cool. He flagged a cab and gave the driver his destination. The metropolitan area, the focus of political, cultural, and financial endeavors, seethed with more than twenty million people. Set out in a series of geometric patterns, the streets were an interlocking mess of intersecting avenues.

Mexico City celebrated contrasts. Hotel and shopping districts catered to tourist crowds. Street vendors littered the thoroughfares. The fragrance of steaming hot tamales and roasted chicken teased his taste buds. As they turned toward the freeway, they drove past a man hawking sweet mangos, the fruit slivered into spears and served in newspaper funnels. For the first time in months Savio's mouth watered. The regular offerings of hand-made dolls, intricately woven wristbands, folded paper flowers, and other colorful trinkets were held up to pedestrians and slow-moving traffic alike. Artisans scraping a living from the largess of tourism lined the busiest boulevards. They passed a horse drawn carriage, once found only in the historic district, as they crept past the ornate façade of an antique church.

The drive took an hour. His accommodations were located at the back of a cul-de-sac in the suburban neighborhood of La Meridad. The villa sat surrounded by homes of impressive scale. The effect spoke more to wealth than taste. Garish statuary and oversized fountains graced most entry paths. Balconies sprouted from each second floor window.

His cover was simple. His ruse as a business consultant in temporary residence would raise no eyebrows. The owner resided in France. This was a supernumerary home of an international investment banker, an association Savio thought offered the additional cachet of universal thievery. Apparently the man only spent brief periods of time in residence. After Savio's first sight of the villa, he hoped support personnel included a housekeeper.

Local landscapers favored gargantuan leaves. Shrubs dwarfed small expanses of verdant green lawn. Fences did not separate the homes from one another and the connected yards provided belts of greenery to bridge each mini estate. There was an unexpected openness to the view.

Every car in sight was expensive, a mixture of American and European models. The neighborhood looked pristine and opulent. Savio knew it for a lie. He'd done as much research as he could manage in the previous week. The manicured surface disguised an enclave of professional thieves, men and women who worked both sides of the legal profession.

His presence would incite little curiosity. A cab in this neighborhood might be unique enough to draw attention but not for long. In the late afternoon light, the lime green and white paint job made the vehicle as much a visible blight as the checkered yellow cabs back in Southern California.

He paid the driver. The walk to the front door was short. A large portico filled the middle of the structure. He stepped under a mass of green vines with white flowers dripping in a cascade of blooms over the top edge. One of his keys unlocked the front door. He stepped over the threshold and entered his new home.

First impressions were critical. Savio paused to let the atmosphere wash in. The entry offered a distinct flavor of a man who favored wealth and considered himself an elite member of society. He passed through the foyer. Fine furnishings and quality art graced the rooms. Though uninhabited, the interior appeared pristine. No dust lingered, no faint footprints trailed over the shiny floors. Despite the lack of visible neglect, there was an undertone of staleness. The house had been shuttered for a length of time before his arrival.

An empty home, even in a neighborhood so refined, invited unwanted guests. He located the alarm panel and typed in the code he'd been provided. The system had three lights on the front plate. The middle one was bright yellow. After he disarmed the alarm it shifted to the left and turned green.

His footsteps sounded heavy as he passed from tile to hardwood floors. The rooms where a family might gather to spend time laughing and visiting were all carpeted. The place was huge. A stealthy individual could reside undetected for months if they kept a low profile. Somebody must pay a healthy amount to keep the estate in such pristine condition. Henri had said the owner traveled, no doubt avoiding extradition. Savio explored the entire villa, each room as fine as those in which he'd spent his youth. From a young age he'd learned to slip in and out of dark bedrooms when visiting dignitaries came to the capital city with daughters in tow. No wonder his father had been such a stickler for decorum.

Many of the upstairs rooms offered bare amenities, as if they'd never been intended for occupation. Out of sight of public eyes, three of the back bedrooms contained oddments of furniture, perhaps the remnants of a designer's makeover.

He moved into the master bedroom. The closet and bureau were filled with the owner's clothing. Other temporary residents might have come and gone but they hadn't disturbed much. Designed to house many people, the villa gave off a vibe as if encouraging treasured guests to extend their stay. A swimming pool graced the backyard. The walled courtyard he'd expected to find, a mainstay of Mexican architecture, was absent. The landscape opened wide, accessible to all.

He showered off the dirt of commercial airline travel. Wrapped in a towel, he cleared a section of clothes rod and transferred his wardrobe. The empty suitcase stowed under the shirt rack, he selected comfortable casual wear for an evening in. A search of the kitchen turned up three key fobs. One set matched those he'd been provided so he tucked them deep inside one of the food cabinets. The next collection looked to open storage cupboards or garden sheds. He hung them back on the hook. The last set contained car keys.

A swift search took him through a door into a connected garage. Inside sat a black Porsche. *Convenient.* Now he would not need to acquire a vehicle. Whether or not the use of the homeowner's car was part of the deal, Savio considered this a handy discovery, one he intended to capitalize on.

The ignition rolled in a sluggish grind before the engine

caught and roared to life. He let the vehicle idle and looked around the space. Not an object askew. Everything was neat and clean. He found no sense of the man who called this home. Not that personality mattered overmuch. The person who exhibited such excellent taste in furnishings and artistry wouldn't leave a fine automobile without connecting a trickle charge unit to the battery. Either the homeowner had left town and been delayed for an extended period, was more careless than signs indicated, or someone had prevented his return.

*Dead*, was Savio's first guess.

He raised the garage door a foot to avoid accidental asphyxiation while he searched for listening devices in the house. By the time he finished the survey he'd found six. *Six.* That leaned toward the overkill end of the spectrum. Persons unknown wanted to hear every word the occupants had to say. He wondered, were they interested specifically in Savio Mendes or in any resident? It appeared he should learn more about the man whose house he occupied.

He scrounged food from the stores in the kitchen cabinets and ate at the breakfast bar. Unpacking his rugged military grade laptop, he connected to the secure remote satellite link and accessed his office computer. He searched for details in the company archives and found the information he wanted attached to the Almeida dossier. The name Marco Fillone was listed on the deed. A Google search turned up several potential candidates but the investment banker under indictment in Mexico jumped off the page as the most probable candidate.

Fillone must have scooted out of town before the Federales came to inquire about his questionable finances. For Savio, this information provoked another question – who paid the gardener and the electric bill?

The doorbell rang.

He closed the internet connection and lowered the cover on his laptop. The remains of his meal abandoned on the counter, he padded barefoot across the floor. His step faltered when he caught sight of three men through the sidelight window and despite deep misgivings, he opened the door.

Eduardo Almeida stood on the step.

Flanked on either side by his security detail, the local dignitary studied him, features displaying no emotion. The two burly guards in grey suits swiveled hard implacable faces as alert eyes searched the rooms beyond the open door. Guns at the ready, they waited for instructions.

Almeida's lips curved into a satisfied bow. "Good evening, Mr. Mendes."

*Fuck. And somebody's cover is blown.*

Fast on his mental feet, Savio hesitated less than a second but the pause was long enough to indicate his surprise. With a flourish, he invited the man and his entourage into the house.

"Welcome, Señor Almeida, to my temporary home."

Almeida walked past him. He dismissed his guard detail with the flick of one hand. He inclined his head, a graceful mannerism for a man of such blocky proportions. "Gracias. You know who I am."

Savio stepped back to keep distance between himself and the intrusive trio. Almeida was a small man by comparison to the goons with their physically imposing presence. Then again, Savio was not a large man either and getting the job done had never been a problem for him. This was not supposed to happen. No direct contact. Nobody expected Almeida to arrive at his fucking front door. His mind raced over data, flipped through the pages of the dossier he'd studied in L.A.

"Of course." He agreed because the statement had not held a note of question. "Your prestige and importance is well-known."

Almeida appeared amused. A square man in a very expensive suit, he wore handcrafted shoes. Although not attractive in the sense of popular fashion, he had all the hallmarks of power and authority.

*A dangerous adversary.*

"May I offer you a drink?" Savio ignored the hired help and motioned in the direction of the salon.

The drug lord inclined his head and indicated he proceed toward the rear of the house.

Savio steered the group toward the salon, the more formal of the rooms.

"Your candor impresses me, Señor. I'm not fond of deceit." Almeida selected a chair that placed his back to a wall and sat.

The smirk lingering around his mouth told Savio that last statement was a lie. The guards assumed positions at either end of the room. Savio padded to the sidebar, poured a drink, and carried the glass to his guest.

After pouring his own glass, Savio took a seat a short distance away. No need to make anyone nervous. "What can I do for you, Señor Almeida?"

Almeida swirled the amber liquid in his glass and sniffed at the cognac. "A fine blend." His gaze settled on Savio. "You understand that I know who you are. My sister lives next door and so I have a particular interest in who resides here."

*Beautiful.*

"Understandable." He took a drink, tempted to toss back the entire contents. Essential information had been omitted from the dossier. Like the fact his next door neighbor was Almeida's sibling.

Savio feared he'd been sold out by someone higher in the food chain. That or this fiasco was the product of career-ending ineptness. Not his – which didn't matter because he would be too dead to enjoy the job security.

Almeida leaned forward to stare at him. "You can imagine my surprise, my pleasure, when I discovered your unusual skills."

Savio's tension relaxed a fraction. His guest referred to the manufactured history the company had designed for him at the time of hire, a precaution in case someone went digging. Almeida had.

"As it turns out, I am in need of a man with your unique talents."

*Unexpected.*

Savio had no plan to get involved. His assignment excluded personal contact and he tried to follow the rules. Mostly. There'd also been Cole's admonishment to avoid attracting undue attention.

*Penalty flag.*

Cole had actually said something along the lines of "don't out your presence in the vicinity of known cartel members."

*Foiled again.*

"Have you met the homeowner?" Almeida swirled a stubby index finger to indicate the room.

Savio frowned and shook his head. "I acquired a short-term lease for the duration of my business."

There was no surprise in Almeida's features. With another flick of his wrist he indicated the guards should exit. The men obeyed. They were clearly paid to listen and not think.

Savio carried his glass over to the credenza for a refill. He hoped Fillone had left a substantial supply of liquor hidden somewhere in the house. He lifted the bottle of port wine, a Portuguese make with a hint of smokiness, and presented the label for his guest's approval. "May I freshen your drink, Señor?"

Almeida held out his glass. He waited until Savio resumed his seat. "I need to know Fillone's location."

Savio swirled his alcohol, sniffed at the fumes and took a swallow before he replied. "The owner will not be in residence for some time. I have taken a six month lease."

"I have personal business with Fillone." Almeida's voice sharpened and he made a visible effort to relax. "I will be open with you. My sister is the daughter of my father's second marriage." He drained his glass.

Savio worked out the relationship. He grasped the connection but not the reason Almeida was here. He rose to do refills again.

Almeida accepted the third drink with a welcome expression. "She always emphasizes she is but half my sibling. Half, whole – I do not understand this pre-occupation with parts. We are family."

Savio conjectured the sister might differentiate because she wished she wasn't related by even half a parent. Interested in surviving this meeting, he refrained from suggesting the idea.

Almeida smiled over the rim of his glass. "I believe you can assist me with a task."

The sight chilled Savio. He interjected a comment. "As I mentioned, I'm in town on business. My schedule is impacted. I have no method to contact Fillone but can supply the information for the rental agency."

Almeida waved away his offer. "Nonsense. There is always time to do a favor for a new friend."

*Tricky bastard.*

With a finger pointed at him, Almeida continued. "You have special skills, Mr. Mendes. I requested a background check on you. I want you to use your experiences and abilities to locate my niece. Such a small task is surely no great challenge for a man of your immense accomplishments." He raised his brows as the sentence ended on a quizzical note.

Savio kept his features neutral. The mixture of truth and falsehoods in his history provided enough details for Almeida to believe he hired out as an enforcer of sorts.

"Aurelia has run away. She is difficult. Too smart for her age." He grimaced. "My sister asks me to intervene."

Savio studied Almeida's face. "A runaway child is not my normal sort of task."

"Consider my request a way to prove you have no loyalty to Fillone." The threat contrasted with Almeida's next hesitation. "That monster is responsible for far more—"

Alarms blasted in Savio's head. This was not the kind of situation an experienced insertion team could miss. Somebody had screwed up. Every company had green recruits but missing these kinds of details defied possibility. No way had this happened by chance. Was he being hung out to dry? He wasn't sure which scenario pissed him off the most.

Almeida mistook his expression as a sign of sympathy. "Aurelia was fourteen when the abuse started."

Savio's attention swiveled back to the conversation.

"Barely a teenager, still a child." Almeida's voice cracked.

Predatory senses came online and Savio's focus sharpened. "Fillone attacked your niece?"

Almeida's eyes watered but he nodded. "Si. The abuse went on for months before my sister learned of the tragedy. Aurelia was fourteen. Still a girl but her body matures into that of a woman. Now, she carries Fillone's bastard."

Savio didn't know what to say. "I am sorry, Señor."

Almeida glared at him. "She did not invite his advances."

Savio dropped his gaze. "Of course not." He chose his next

words with care. "I believe grown men should not be distracted by youths who play dress-up in their mother's clothes and cosmetics."

He'd seen girls made into women too soon and the reality angered him. The world was difficult for most females. Opportunities lacked in employment and basic education. Had his mother not been guarded by mentors and tutors, her talent nurtured and supported, she might have fallen prey to such a predator.

Savio tilted his head to one side and stared at Eduardo Almeida. Tension ratcheted as the silence lengthened.

Almeida extracted a cigarette and lit the tip. He sucked hard and expelled a cloud of smoke before he spoke again. "I need your assistance. I hire investigators to find my niece. Aurelia eludes them. She makes them look like foolish puppies." He shrugged but a hint of a prideful smile curved his lips.

"Today's youth are clever." Savio said, adopting a neutral tone.

"Perhaps I should send her to school, rather than Rodrigo, eh? He has no head for figures. Instead, he spends too much money on clothes and women." The man darted a glance at Savio's face and found polite disinterest. "Rodrigo is my younger brother. Someday, he will share in the control of Almeida Enterprises. If, that is, he ever grows up."

The last was muttered more to himself than proffered for conversation so Savio ignored it.   Relaxed against the back of his chair, he maintained a careful expression of civility. He recognized the name. Rodrigo attended a prestigious American university, the golden child of the Almeida brood. More than a decade younger than Eduardo, the youngest sibling had been raised in an atmosphere of wealth and privilege.

First, the company had screwed Savio with a lousy set-up.

Now, Almeida wanted to crawl in bed together. An opportunity like this was comparable to a celestial alignment and happened about as often. He could no more pass up the chance to ride in Almeida's breast pocket than Henri would turn down a promotion. If he proved successful, Aurelia's recovery and return home might make the topmost tier of the cartel beholden to him. *Sold.*

He brought the conversation back around to Almeida's request. "What do you think I can do for you?"

"You solve problems – accomplish what no one else can seem to manage." Almeida's amusement drained away. "Aurelia has not even experienced her *quinceañera*. Like all girls today, she looks much older. She is intractable, rebellious." He frowned down into his drink. "She spends time in the seediest parts of downtown, calls herself Palenque."

Savio digested this information. For a man like Almeida, his niece's fifteenth birthday celebration would be as much a gala event as a society wedding. Not only had the girl brought dishonor to the family through Fillone's actions, but she'd compromised an event designed to showcase Almeida's social status in the community. Not to mention that the use of a street name usually meant a person was accepted and blended into the community. Aurelia might be a true woman of the streets by now. Palenque was a prehistoric ruin, an ancient city in southern Mexico. He'd seen the remnants of the tallest temple once during a reconnaissance flight. He made a mental note to Google for other associations.

With a curt nod he committed himself. "Of course, I am pleased to offer my assistance. I will locate your niece." He let some of his disgust show. "And I will endeavor to learn more about Fillone. A man who takes advantage of a child deserves harsh treatment."

Almeida leaned forward, his face tipped into the light cast by the table lamp. "I intend to see him punished." The words were more effective for the lack of inflection.

Accepting this task meant placing himself in the man's hip pocket, privy to his personal thoughts. The chance offered the connection deep cover intelligence operatives spent months, even years, developing. A fortuitous opportunity that had landed on Savio's doorstep, literally, and which meant Almeida intended to kill him post-delivery. Since the original focus of his visit to Mexico was intel, Savio would accomplish that from a closer and more personal viewpoint. This job was all about the ability to capitalize on opportunity. Example in point – installed for mere hours, his ruse had already derailed. Almeida had wired the house, collected advance information on the new occupant, investigated his background, and taken advantage.

Score one for the bad guys.

In deliberate mimicry, Savio clasped his palms together in a posture of prayer. Although separated by several yards of carpeted floor, he stared into the other man's eyes with intensity. "I will need current photographs and video content, if available. A detailed list of her habits, friends or family members she contacts, and any places she frequents. That's enough to get started."

Almeida's eyes reflected lamplight.

The man seldom blinked. The quirk might indicate the influence of some narcotic but Savio thought not. The fold of the lid functioned to wick moisture across the surface of the eye. Given the watery glisten, the man only needed to blink half as often as the rest of humanity. Instead of a limpid, sorrowful expression, the wet orbs increased the intensity of his stare.

With a suddenness that caught him off guard, Almeida relaxed. "We have an accord, Mr. Mendes. You may see my sister in the morning to review the necessary materials."

Almeida swirled his drink. The amber liquid turned fiery in the subdued light. An indefinable quality of charisma lent him an attraction, even when you knew he was a monster. Such a man should not be underestimated.

"I select my clients based on what they can afford to pay but in your case, Señor Almeida, I will undertake this task because I have morals." Savio tilted his glass in an indistinct salute and drained the contents. The port was smooth and warm, not unpleasant to his palate.

Almeida retained his serious expression. "I too have ethics, Señor Mendes."

Ironic amusement tickled Savio, now there was an intriguing and perhaps pointless difference.

# CHAPTER THREE

SAVIO PUNCHED THE hanging bag, one dull thud after another. He did it again, continuing until his knuckles ached and rivulets of sweat streamed down the hard contours of his chest. Fingers stiff and pectoral muscles straining, he slumped forward and sucked in deep breaths. The home gym at the rear of the house helped work off his frustrated energy. Every ten blows he alternated primary position, feet relocated to absorb maximum impact. Boxing had never been a favorite pastime but he enjoyed the flex and pull of muscles and the sting of each hard strike.

Almeida's departure left Savio in an emotional vacuum. He was torn between elation over the invitation to swim in the deep end of the pool and remorse for his disregarded orders. Even though he couldn't have avoided contact unless he'd ignored answering the door, he debated what the turn of events might cost him. After rehabilitation and his subsequent dismissal from the military, he'd landed in the private security sector. A dismal time in his life compared to his current position. Though grateful to Henri, once he'd proved himself he hadn't needed anyone's vote of confidence. The company had been thrilled with his rate of success.

This time his deep cover had taken an unexpected turn. This had to work and he was motivated to succeed, thus, the deal with Eduardo Almeida. Should Aurelia prove a thorn in her uncle's side, Savio planned to twist the barb through the man's ribs. And he might smile while he did it.

In places where education and opportunity were restricted to those with wealth or resources, success for women came under few headings. Most fell under two categories – hard choices and narrow routes to the top. Treated and discarded as sexual commodities among both the poorest and wealthiest of settings, he didn't blame any female who used her assets to get ahead. Some needn't rely on their beauty or offer up their bodies to secure a place in the world but too many did. Add in the volatility of the drug trade and tragedy abounded. If Aurelia leveraged pressure well enough to manipulate her uncle, Savio saw no fault in her methods, but he still needed to find her.

Savio added the girl's name to his mental list. The space was getting crowded with Almeida and Fillone already waiting for vetting.

Henri's lack of candor put him in a precarious place. Field operatives struggled with trust issues. In his chosen industry, one mistake and it was game over. He could think of no reason for why Henri kept him in the dark. Even so, the fact rankled. There was no logic in leaving him ignorant of Almeida's connection to the house next door. The man's unexpected appearance on his doorstep could have proved lethal. Might still.

The thought made him pause. He panted for air, arms loose at his sides and fingers flexed.

Henri didn't benefit from Savio's death; at least not in any discernible way. That path soon ran out of steam and expired. Other than a shared language and service in the same military, he and Henri had few interests in common. They did not socialize outside of work or frequent similar entertainments. All of which equaled zero value for Henri in the deception. Unless, the discrepancy came from elsewhere in the company? The other operatives kept low profiles, just as he did. He knew some by name and most by face, but they avoided friendships. Solitude served a primary need. Trust was hard to establish, an occupational hazard. You didn't survive long in this profession if you trusted indiscriminately.

Frustrated with the lack of answers he pounded the bag until his knuckles ached. Physical exertion pushed aside numbness. Pain registered. He moved on to his regular routine of stretching. Even one day without a workout resulted in tight muscles around the taut scars on his thigh. Despite the grim expectations of doctors, he'd recovered his complete range of motion. But no matter how much he exercised or trained, that leg always flagged first. In his mind the barely discernible hesitation stood out liked a parade banner, a weakness identified and capitalized upon by any alert enemy.

Running worked off emotional turmoil but a jog through the unfamiliar neighborhood was inadvisable this evening. No collateral damage on his menu tonight.

He double-checked the locks on all the doors and reset the alarm. A wasted gesture since Almeida probably had a spare set of keys. Hell, the bastard could have installed the security system. Savio shrugged it off. Short of sleeping inside a locked closet or finding a hotel, events would transpire at will.

Laptop retrieved from the kitchen counter, he snagged a bottle of water from the fridge and climbed the stairs. A quick survey of home security options helped him decide to sleep with the Heckler and Koch under his pillow. The lock on the master suite didn't inspire confidence. Neither did the one on the entrance to the bathroom and he'd already been surprised once tonight. Handgun within easy reach, he indulged in a hot shower. Afterward, he crawled into bed, skin still damp, and let the 1200 thread-count sheets soak up the moisture. Eyelids at half-mast, he found it hard to imagine he'd boarded the flight from Los Angeles only that morning. In less than twelve hours he'd blown his cover and made direct contact with his quarry. Or, vice versa.

And don't forget, he'd been offered and accepted new employment. *Awkward.* That must set a record of some kind. He'd confess all to Henri on his first check-in. Certain he'd earn an ass-chewing for events that were essentially outside his control, he was content to postpone the news. Maybe he'd report to Cole instead, get fired, and just disappear into the landscape.

An hour later a noise wakened him.

Climbing out of bed, he staggered to the window and peered outside. The clock hadn't even turned midnight but a shadow crept from shrub to tree trunk. *Amateur.* The bent-over figure darted like a ludicrous cartoon thief in a child's animated movie. An overturned deck chair sprawled beside the pool, probably the noise that woke him. The culprit again lurched through the night. Amusement curved Savio's mouth. He'd caught sight of the over-sized handgun clutched in the intruder's right hand. Dirty Harry had arrived.

He pulled on a pair of sweats and trotted down the main staircase, eyes scanning outside the windows until he pinpointed the visitor near the foundation. The stranger gazed up at the second-story balcony of the master suite.

The lock made a soft click when Savio turned the knob. There was no change in his late night guest's demeanor, so he eased open one of the patio doors and stepped out on the tiled expanse. The ceramic was cold underfoot. The uneven surface provided rough traction against the soles of his bare feet. The garden lights were placed in strategic locations, most of which had been shut off by an automatic system. The few lit ones shone where a late night arrival might walk. In the reflected light Savio identified the figure as a young man. The profile of the gun he carried showed an antiquated pistol. A bullet fired through a barrel corroded from disuse would be dangerous, more so for the shooter. For a few seconds Savio studied the scene. Youthful and armed, the miscreant skulked around the outside of Fillone's home with a purpose. He'd bet a silver dollar this kid led in a straight line back to Aurelia.

He crossed the tiles, stepped on the grass and snagged the boy in a headlock. Disarmed with a twist of the wrist, he clamped a hand across the boy's mouth and cut off a high-pitched squeak of shock. He dragged the prisoner inside the house before they attracted attention. Savio was certain Almeida had stationed a man in the perimeter between here and his sister's home. The boy struggled, flailing his hands until his fingers found purchase and wrapped around Savio's wrist. He tried to pry away the blockage that constricted his air. Savio tightened his arm in response and the boy's brief panic subsided into submission.

He hauled the boy through the kitchen, stopped to grab the car keys from the hook, and continued out into the garage. At the passenger side he whispered in his ear. "Make no sounds. Your life depends on it."

An abbreviated nod of agreement came quick.

Savio stretched and opened the door, then shoved the disarmed intruder inside and pushed it shut. He rounded the front bumper and dropped the clunky gun on the workbench.

The boy stared at him through the windshield, eyes wide and frightened. His prominent Adam's apple bobbed as he swallowed.

Good. Nervous meant cooperation would be forthcoming. Savio paused at the driver's side and held a finger up to his lips to indicate his continued desire for silence. He waited until he got it and then opened the door and slid into the seat.

"What are—"

He silenced the passenger with a dark look, inserted the key and turned the ignition. Fillone's car might also be bugged but he guessed a GPS device was more probable. At least that's what he would do. Tomorrow he'd conduct a thorough search before he left the house.

Savio looked at his companion. No more than sixteen, the boy was dressed in cheap pants and a ragged t-shirt, his feet falling out of a worn pair of flimsy sandals, the type farmers often wore. "Who are you?"

A sullen face stared at him.

"Answer my questions with clarity or I will break your fingers one at a time."

The boy roused, a flash of ire on display. He'd been caught red-handed and hadn't the smarts to know he was in a bad situation.

"You are not Fillone. I came to shoot that bastard."

*Ah, another one.* "Why?"

Cheeks flushed red as if with fever, the boy's nostrils flared, the nares wide as passion erupted. "He is despicable. He deflowered Aurelia."

The girl's name rolled off his tongue like music. The sounds flowed from his lips and Savio heard the impassioned speech of a boy in the throes of infatuation. Great, maybe Romeo knew where to find Juliet.

"What is your name?"

"Enrique."

"I will deal with Fillone, but I need to speak to Aurelia, on behalf of her family. I must see her. Help me to make contact. I'll provide my information."

"Why are we in the car?"

"Because no one can hear us in here."

The boys eyes widened until white shone all around his pupils.

Savio continued. "Aurelia's uncle is concerned for her welfare. He has taken steps to find her. Go home, Enrique. Leave this task to the professionals. Tell Aurelia I can provide whatever she needs. Bring her to me. I want to help." He thought the speech was smart but he couldn't say if anything had gotten through to Enrique.

"Fillone must pay for what he has done."

"He will." A safe promise.

"I'm not afraid of you."

"Of course not." He agreed.

Savio did not smile but he wanted to. Had he ever been so young and transparent? Probably. And he would not have appreciated any adult telling him such an evident truth. Enrique was a man but much of the boy still clung to his spare frame. If he grew into his lanky height and filled out, he would boast a physique that rivaled an athlete. Right now he looked half comical with his knees hoisted up in the low-slung seat, back stiff, and lower lip out-thrust.

Enrique jabbed a finger in the air. "Aurelia's uncle doesn't care about what happens to her. All he wants is power and money." The words were spoken with the fervor of someone who lived through hunger and gone without medicine.

Savio considered what he knew before asking the obvious question. "Why would Eduardo Almeida lack concern for his sister's daughter?"

The boy slumped back in the seat. "He has no respect for anyone, women especially. His sister is just a commodity he manipulates."

Savio heard the difference in cadence. The lilt to the boys Spanish indicated a trace of one of the indigenous languages of Mexico, probably Nahuatl, considering the outlying communities. Same as in his native Brazil, most of the populous spoke a common language with regional differences. An attenuated ear could discern the inflections and identify the vicinity. He could not.

"Explain."

The boy looked mutinous but responded to the directive. "Aurelia's mom is from a village near El Popo. You know, Popocatépetl, the smoking mountain." He pointed toward the front of the house.

Savio nodded. "I know it's a volcano, nevermind the geography lesson."

Enrique shrugged. "Aurelia and me, we grew up together. Almeida came and took them away two years ago. Now he uses their connection to funnel his poison to the fields."

"You followed her to the city?"

"She sent me a message. She asked for my help." His chest bellowed out. "I came because I love her."

"Of course." This time he was unable to hide the delight in his pronouncement. "So why would Eduardo Almeida want to harm his niece?"

The boy clamped his mouth shut.

Savio lifted Enrique's hand. "Which finger shall I start with?"

As if the motion sucked out his resistance, the boy's composure deflated and the fear returned. "Aurelia dreams of freedom."

"Exactly how would she achieve such freedom?"

"She has a plan to destroy her uncle." Enrique added a nod for emphasis.

Savio was tired. He wanted to climb back into bed and sleep. "It has been a long day for me, Enrique. Perhaps we might discuss the particulars before I lose patience and forget about breaking fingers and instead move on to your neck."

"She works with her uncle, the younger one. I don't know the details." The boy eyed him with a worried frown. "I don't."

That might be true. Regardless, this was a link. "How do I find Aurelia."

Enrique's shoulders rounded down. "I do not know." His whisper carried a note of sadness. "She will not tell me. I leave a message at the photo shop on Calle Mañana and she calls me."

"Give me your cell phone." He ignored the boy's blank expression and held out his hand. After a brief delay Enrique's mouth screwed up into a grimace and he pulled one from his pants pocket. Savio typed and saved his own number under the name Palenque and handed the phone back. "Tell Aurelia to call me. The search for her will not cease. Her uncle won't allow her to escape."

Enrique's hand disappeared into the folds of his shirt." Can I have my gun back?"

"No. Get out of the vehicle and exit through the house. Do not speak. Do not be seen. Disappear. If you lurk in my greenery again, I will hurt you first and ask questions later." He tapped the boy on the side of the head for emphasis. Not hard enough to bruise, but with force that indicated serious intent.

Enrique was young. He took offense but he also knew when to keep his mouth shut.

Savio followed him as far as the shadows on the patio and watched him disappear into the foliage. Then he locked up the house for the second time and stomped back upstairs. He'd just crawled between the sheets when his phone beeped. He groaned. Had Aurelia hidden in the yard and waited for her compatriot? They were children – of course she might have. He ignored the notification but a lingering sense of duty roused him from lethargy. If Almeida's niece reached out, he could at least answer the call.

He grabbed the phone and tapped in his access code, swiped a finger across the screen. A text from Henri.

*Report.*

Savio rolled over and stared at the ceiling. Crap. Henri wanted a preliminary assessment. On his first day in the field, the request felt pushy. He was tempted to ignore the message. Unwise. He debated how to respond and waffled about whether or not he should explain the change in his circumstances. The face-to-face meeting with Almeida complicated his job. If Savio indicated no unusual events and Henri suspected otherwise, he'd tip his hand. The reverse also held true. If he admitted business had gone awry, the company might yank him home to L.A. The image of his office and desk made the decision for him, there was no place better than the field. He texted a response.

*Unexpected contact. Tertiary informant. Site not secure.*

With several ways to interpret his terse comments he hoped Henri puzzled over them. He didn't. The answer came less than a minute later.

*Proceed as planned.*

What did that mean? A scowl tightened the skin on his forehead. An uncharacteristic headache blossomed. His original task as silent observer crashed and burned the moment he cracked the door to Almeida. Business could not proceed as usual.

He returned the phone to the bedside table and flopped back on the pillows. He uttered a dismissive snort. If the start to this job was any indication of how things would *proceed* he might as well commit to a solo operation right now. His level of confidence in the company had been shaken to the foundation. From here on out he expected diminished returns. He turned his back to the wall and with one hand under the pillow beside the gun, he closed his eyes. After this night, sleep seemed like a gift.

# CHAPTER FOUR

THE NEXT MORNING Savio observed Eduardo Almeida's arrival. The sleek black car cruised to a stop in the circular driveway of the sister's house. From his vantage point through the downstairs window he watched as the driver remained seated behind the wheel. Almeida must be in the back on the phone. Today Savio's goal was the extraction of more details about the niece. He wasn't without skill in locating missing persons but as a stranger he lacked access to the underground network through which data streamed. The rate news could travel from mouth-to-mouth on the street rivaled sophisticated communication systems. He needed an entry point, some bit of information hidden inside the useless details the mother or uncle knew.

Almeida exited the vehicle. Dressed in an off-white linen

suit he should have appeared comical but the set of his shoulders evidenced an indefinable power. He disappeared through the front door, both bodyguards in tow.

For a moment, Savio considered probabilities. Could the company not have identified the neighbor as Eduardo Almeida's sister? Few Americans grasped how naming conventions differed in Hispanic communities. Women and men seldom shared the same surname. Honest mistakes happened. Even so, he dismissed the idea. No such error could slip through a proper screen. In fact, the reverse was more apt to be true. The banker's home had been selected for its proximity to a primary family member. Which then raised the question of who removed the banker and had it been done for Savio's installation?

Information had been withheld. And he did not know why or if it had been deliberate.

He adjusted the loose fit of the guayabera shirt and smiled. Fillone's closet pleased his sense of style. The pale blue fabric, embroidered with flowers, embodied a flavor of traditional Mexico he much enjoyed. Naked without the Heckler and Koch tucked under his shoulder, he stepped outside. No point going armed when Almeida's goons would remove his weapon. He hated strangers touching his gun.

Almeida speared his fingers through his hair. He gazed at Savio with a sorrowful face. "I did not know she was going to have a child until recently. Now Aurelia's shame is a blemish on my honor, one that cannot be made right."

They sat at a table in a den off the main entry, photographs spread over the surface.

Savio was confused by the man's statement. Did Almeida mean his niece's unwanted pregnancy was more offensive than the abuse the girl had suffered by Fillone? Either way, Almeida's priorities were screwed up. The arrival of a woman in a household uniform saved him from the need to make a comment.

She set down a beverage tray and exited the room without a sound. The sister's house was formal to a fault, the feudal class system alive and well in Mexico. He busied himself and poured coffee.

Almeida tidied his ruffled head. "Forgive my theatrics. I struggle with this situation." He accepted the cup and took a sip.

Savio studied him. He couldn't decide if the man's obvious distress stemmed from genuine concern about his niece's welfare or from some other unknown source.

"She is pretty, right?" Almeida pushed another photo across the polished surface of the table.

The girl was striking. In his adopted town of Los Angeles, her features were on par with models and actors, though at just shy of five feet tall her lack of height might ruin any chance of serious success in those industries. Hollywood types preferred long legs.

Savio set down his coffee. "You said there are files?" So far all he'd seen were the photographs.

"Si. I will have a courier deliver them to you. I did not visit the office before we met." He motioned at the pictures. "These are copies my sister made. There are more in the files. I used two different investigators. Failures, both of them." He snapped off the words.

Clearly, disappointing Eduardo Almeida was a bad idea. "You will be pleased with my results, Señor."

Almeida stared at him for a few seconds, and then nodded, the movement slow and thoughtful. "I believe you, Mr. Mendes."

Savio turned his focus back to the photographs and selected one. In this snapshot the girl's head tilted to one side, her face angled downward so when the photographer had asked for her attention, she appeared to look up. Eyes luminous and dark, he sensed the same inherent force of character in the man across from him. Like uncle, like niece. If Aurelia grew into that promise she would be a strong and beautiful woman. A notion he tucked away for later consideration. He sorted through the spread of pictures again until he found an image offering a straight-on view of her angular face. He wanted a photo to show people, to shake loose a new lead.

"How long ago was this one taken?" He turned it to the other man could see.

"My sister's birthday party last November."

Good. Less than six months old. He liked this one because he fancied he could see a hint of the woman Aurelia was destined to become. A layer of maturity hovered over her image like a superimposed ghost of the future. And if she appeared older than her numerical years, as girls too often did at fourteen, the picture might better resemble her present appearance.

"Should I enjoy your success in this endeavor, Mr. Mendes, we will discuss further business opportunities."

Savio smiled with genuine pleasure. So the head of the cartel wanted to plumb his talents. Fine with him. "I look forward to our discussion. You should know I generally consult on matters of business involving the removal of competitors."

"Yes." Almeida's single word held a wealth of information and intimidation.

Either Almeida knew more about Savio's background than what the company's standard biography offered or he'd inferred as much. Not such a stretch considering his profession.

The drug dealer leaned forward and set down his coffee cup.

His gaze locked on Savio. "I want you to find Aurelia." The man's face became taut. "I cannot return her stolen childhood but I will not have her baby born in the gutter." The open display of emotion, though unexpected, appeared sincere.

An uncomfortable foreboding came over Savio. Last night, the explanation of Fillone's culpability rang with the certainty of truth. Today, Almeida's tone held an off-kilter note.

Almeida shifted in his chair and swiveled to prop one ankle across a knee. "Aurelia deserves the future I can offer." He waved his hands in a gesture of frustration. "These young people today—I don't understand them. She listens to angry music and dresses like a homeless person."

Disaffected youth told the same story everywhere. Savio leaned forward, his mouth lean and expression hard. "I will find your niece, Señor. Now then, let us talk of compensation."

Savio needed information from Henri. If he asked the right question, the answer might indicate which side of the deck had dealt this hand of cards. He'd maybe identify who most benefited from playing this game. And he wanted out of Fillone's house. The constant pressure of scrutiny in every sound recorded, weighed on him.

A fast drive relieved stress and provided freedom to speak. Win. Win. He looked forward to hitting the road. A thorough search of the vehicle produced a GPS tracker. A close inspection of the small electronic dot showed it was the same model he used. He had no way of knowing if it was company-issued and after a short debate, he decided to leave it in place. Maybe the company wanted to keep tabs on his driving. Either there was no microphone in place or he'd missed it in his survey, in which case Almeida had already heard about Enrique's visit. That negated the need to be careful what he said inside the car.

The Porsche's leather interior dragged him back in time to his first experience behind the wheel. Savio still recalled the excited flutter of anticipation deep in his stomach. At twelve he'd been small for his age and his foot strained to reach the accelerator pedal. This car also smelled of leather and polish, a pleasant combination lacking only the faint trace of his father's cigar smoke. Even now the memory tasted of pungent Cuban tobacco, the reason his mother forbade the odor inside her home. A pang of regret stung him. He recalled the way the scent of lemon and almonds clung to his mother's skin, sweet from the cakes and cookies she baked. The memory of her loss still burned although a dozen years had passed, her death another chasm between him and his surviving parent.

His mother had taught him to dance but his father had given him the gift of absence. Savio had followed the paternal footsteps and spent most of his adult life in absentia. First in the military, he'd let missions and expectations consume a decade. After the explosion that left him injured, hospitals and rehabilitation had consumed another year. Then he'd drifted into private security. Now he lived the life of a minor diplomat like his parents had always wanted. Except his existence was a lie. He didn't work for any government. This wasn't even his country. Things only looked as though they'd come full circle. He still lived in isolation. He thrust away the thoughts and the memories, turned the key in the ignition. He had a job to do. He dialed Henri's number as soon as he reached the freeway.

"So it turns out Eduardo Almeida has a half-sister. She lives right next door. I don't understand how the research team missed that nugget but I'm damn near rubbing elbows with the family." He waited for Henri's response.

"I'll have a word with the head of the group."

Not what he expected. No surprise. No shock. No concern

about his welfare. Now Savio questioned if the listening devices inside Fillone's house had been planted by someone other than Almeida.

"This isn't bad information, Savio. Take advantage of this opportunity. Close in on Almeida, earn his confidence, and get him to share details." Henri's voice came forceful through the ear bud.

Traffic opened up. Savio downshifted and accelerated. Henri was out of his mind. The closer he scuttled to Almeida's nest, the flimsier and more precarious his cover story became.

"I am on a first-name basis with the head of the cartel." He paused to let the words sink in. If Almeida ran his business like any other drug lord that would never happen. His rejection of the standard model had been successful. Bolstered along by his willingness to kill anyone who angered him, he removed competitors at a ruthless rate. One day he would alienate the wrong person. Hopefully.

Henri grunted a sound of approval. "Cole's upped the pressure. He's provided a healthy bankroll on this endeavor. We need a return on our investment."

Savio shifted lanes and opened up the Porsche. The tires hugged the pavement as he blew past a flock of sedans and drifted back into the slow lane. He considered what Henri had just said. This operation required seed money, sure, but not a lot. His stint in Nicaragua last year had been useless, thanks to interference by the local branch of the American CIA, and nobody complained then.

"Give me specifics, Henri. I can't collect good data if I don't know what the company is actually after." Nothing was forthcoming. He let the silence build for a few more seconds, and then unleashed some of his frustration. "I'm sanctioned to observe, not interact. I'm right next door to a relative. As a point of contact, I'm in the bastard's pocket and you still won't share why. I'm at risk, Henri. Tell me what we're really after." The absence of sound became a pregnant pause. Traffic ebbed. "Do I need to worry about the owner of the villa showing up and being upset that I've borrowed a shirt or two?"

"No worries there."

Henri's flat voice confirmed his suspicion. Fillone was dead. Everybody had lied. The more he thought about Almeida's story, the less sense his explanation made. He needed an outsider because of the personal nature of his business. The idea was ridiculous. People would see Aurelia's pregnant belly at some point. Did anyone care about a child born out of wedlock today? Even in the most devout Catholic families, a birth was preferential to abortion. He shrugged off those ideas. The man's desire for privacy reflected a concern about his reputation in the community.

Savio veered off the next exit, a random choice. At the end of the ramp, he navigated toward a cluster of retail businesses a short distance down a cross street. Signs promised food and his stomach clenched. He'd forgotten to eat again.

"Give me a reason not to hang up, Henri." He hadn't intended to say the words, but fuck it, why the hell not? He did manage to keep the snarl out of his voice.

Henri's connection crackled. "Engage the network. Infiltrate the ranks for detailed information. Identify the production lines. Track the sources of distribution. This opportunity is a career-maker, son."

Savio bristled at the familiar term, but made a general sound of agreement. At the same time, he tried to decode the mixed messages Henri delivered. First, he'd been instructed to watch. Now, that had switched to engage. The lack of concern about maintaining his cover defied logic. Under normal circumstances risky behavior brought a sense of excitement, but today Savio felt unsettled. The careful collection of intelligence had been bypassed and the urgency that stemmed from Henri's insistence on speed, grated. Objects moving too fast often crashed. Hurrying got people killed. No one enjoyed a thrill ride more than him but Savio was not ready to embrace the ghost. Not yet.

"Go deeper." Henri's voice cut off.

Savio growled. The line was silent. Henri had hung up.

He exited the vehicle and resisted the desire to slam the door. With a quick jerk he removed the ear piece, shoved the length of wire into his front pants pocket and dismantled the cheap throw-away cell phone. He dropped the electronic component through a grate in the street with a twinge of guilt. He'd read about conservation efforts to restore the rivers flowing beneath the concrete layers of the city but in this case, his need for security prevailed. No one could recover an item dropped into the sewage-filled flow. The outer components of the phone he deposited in a trash receptacle outside a small market, one of the corner stores that serviced even the smallest of neighborhoods.

The scent of simple foods teased his nostrils. He sniffed the air with appreciation and he headed for the door of the establishment. He ordered food and drink, settled at a table to one side of the room. He considered what he'd learned since his arrival in Mexico. Intrigue and questions percolated in his brain. Would his backroom deal with Almeida be sanctioned on this job? Being left out of the communication loop stranded him with a dangerous knowledge gap about company goals. Henri's urgent prodding to bypass protocol violated company principles. Either Henri was in over his head or he didn't care about the potential risk to Savio. Neither was good for his longevity.

Despite the escalation of troubles, he would stay because now he needed to know. He'd cultivate his relationship with Almeida and discover Aurelia's hidden location. He'd shake them both until their teeth rattled to get the truth.

# 5 CHAPTER FIVE

Over the next two weeks, Savio lounged away his days in different restaurants and cantinas around the city. He savored the food, indulged in drinking local beer, and read the papers. All the while he eyed the crowd of patrons in each place of business. No one paid him any unusual attention. Under other circumstances he might think that suspicious, but he blended here. He also surveyed Almeida's operations. He spoke with the man on the phone every couple of days, offering candid updates about his activities, none of which had yet to produce results. He imitated a cat playing with a mouse, a predator studying his quarry, and all the while the clock ticked down.

One day, on page three of the local paper, he found a small picture of Eduardo Almeida surrounded by children. Savio read the article with interest. The heavy usage of positive phrases like the "esteemed businessman" in regard to the man's gift of funds for school repairs and library expansion indicated his revered status in the community. The children who attended the educational academy came from families with resources but they did not number among the wealthy. It was shrewd. This circuitous way to recruit favor with local officials and their relatives drew favorable public attention. More good press granted the ability to control the voice of the people. The method worked. Almeida enjoyed a reputation as a concerned professional who utilized his skills and success on behalf of others.

Savio needed additional background on the players in his little drama. He supplemented the information in the dossier with internet research. The amount of data available at the click of a mouse added substantially to the official record provided by the company. Savio liked to know the local setting and in this case his efforts were stymied by Almeida's popularity. People knew what he was but they didn't care because he was better than his predecessors.

Between the information Savio had been issued and what he'd learned on his own, he'd pieced together the extent of the network. The news services and the legal system operated with an awareness of the existence and scope of the various drug consortiums. Governments, officials, and cartel infrastructures connected through an elaborate system of bribery. Almeida had grown his holdings while maintaining a low profile. His reach was impressive. He'd swallowed up smaller distribution networks and allowed gangs of residential tough guys to operate like satellite offices. This decision reduced profit-margins since a percentage of profits were siphoned from the cash flow but built-in intimidation was ready and available when and wherever needed as a result. The out-sourcing implemented an innovative approach to the industry of drug-production and distribution. And it worked.

Almeida's aspirations ranged beyond his backyard. He wanted to go international where the big money existed. Much as a bank operated, he'd established individual lines of credit. He sent delivery couriers out to distant locations with quantities of raw saturated material. Onsite cooks used the pure undiluted content to produce a hundred-fold increase in finished drug product. By comparison to the Columbian cartel pattern, the result might be construed as small potatoes.

Which only demonstrated the intelligence of Almeida's business model.

His cut was profitable and his risk low. His personal investment approached nil. He had a literal factory that produced the stuff in monumental quantities, just like a regular corporate manufacturer. In shorthand, he'd legalized the process through proper channels. Instead of packaging headache pills, he packaged the ephedrine for the creation of methamphetamine and he did it in volume.

The plan was diabolical, brilliant but simple. Masterful. In a way, Savio admired the set up. He also fantasized about shooting Almeida between the eyes. He even pinpointed where he'd place the bullet—just to the left of center in order to perforate the frontal lobe. An unimportant detail since a projectile on either side would end the man's life. Only his desire to learn more kept him from impulsive action.

He believed he'd traced three active outbound routes. The first appeared to terminate in Guatemala. The second arched overseas to Malaysia. The third, the one which made Almeida most happy, led to the United States. In the world of illegal narcotics America still offered the land of greatest opportunity and it was right next door. At first Savio dismissed the drug

trails but as he gathered information he realized they were responsible for a larger degree of the production than initial esti-
mates indicated. He needed to alter his thought processes to
match changes in the industry.

Comfortable in his role, Almeida followed a set routine and
interacted with a regular group of business connections. It made
following him much easier.

Back in Fillone's car, Savio headed for Centro Histórico.
Around him Mexico was busy and industrious. His plan was to
spend the next hour or so tailing Almeida from his office to various points in the city. Displeased with his progress, despite the
details he'd uncovered, Savio had little usable data to pass
along. There had been no further visits from Enrique, no night-
time interruptions to his life. He spent his days in the collection
of information in an attempt to narrow the trail leading to Aurelia's location. At this point he was interested in any open avenue.

His personal cell phone rang. He looked and saw the message for a restricted number. Not Henri. He answered.

"Mendes? It's Cole."

When the head of the company called, a situation unusual
enough to warrant a stab of adrenalin, he listened hard. "Good
afternoon."

"I've been trying to reach Henri for a week. Where he is?"

Surprised, Savio faltered. "Henri is supposed to be in his office in Los Angeles." At least he'd claimed he was there.

Silence met this statement.

"I'm against this kind of infiltration operation, Mendes. The
company doesn't operate this way but I told Henri if you wanted to stick your neck out, then I'd back the play. I need to
know what's happening though and I'm not hearing any expla-
nations. You're out on a limb and that makes me nervous."

Savio frowned. He didn't respond till several seconds had ticked past. "I'm following directives, as ordered, Sir."

Another silence stretched out.

"Cut the crap, Mendes. You're a hothead. Henri put his ass on the line to back you up in this endeavor. Give me some results."

Henri had come to him with this idea, not the other way around.

"Yes, Sir." Savio's tone carried no inflection whatsoever but his mind raced. This time, he let the silence draw out. Something was out of sync. He hadn't been upstairs long enough to know the topography, yet he suspected this wasn't the way the company operated.

He thought he'd caught Cole by surprise. The man spoke again in measured tones. "I see. I want you to report directly to me in this matter, Mendes. Consider that an order. Use the main reception line and request to be put through to my office. I'll expect to hear from you on a seventy-two hour cycle."

"Yes, Sir."

Savio disconnected and held the phone cupped in his hand. Possibilities processed. Cole had been briefed on the mission but his perspective differed from Savio's own instructions. The logical source for the discrepancy weighed on him. Mexico was Henri's playground, the region he'd been assigned for five years.

*Henri recruited me.*

For the first time, he wondered what circumstances lured Henri Cavalleri to the private sector. After Savio had been forced out of the military, all he'd desired was to get back in the field. Maybe the same hadn't been true for Henri. He'd never asked.

This mission was rotten at the core. Savio felt the certainty in his bones. Almeida wasn't the only person being played. He wanted to know if he was a pawn or collateral damage. Had he been recruited as an expendable asset? That stung. He slowed and pulled into the curb a short distance from Almeida's building. His focus now was manipulating the right levers. He'd worry about Henri and Cole later.

He caught sight of Almeida's car pulling out of the lower level garage. He followed the driver to a restaurant and waited ninety minutes. Back in motion, he tracked the black sedan to the tourist district, a strange place for Almeida to venture. His driver double-parked and Savio watched the drug kingpin exit his vehicle and enter a photo shop.

The same photo shop Enrique had mentioned he visited to leave messages for Aurelia? Savio frowned. What could Almeida want in a photography studio unless the business fronted some other enterprise? He left his own vehicle and took up a position against a wall. The afternoon sun canted between the buildings but where he leaned, the shade felt cool.

He pressed his shoulders against the wall of the building and stretched muscles tensed by waiting. He passed time studying the crowd. The flow of lunchtime traffic in the city catered to locals. In the afternoon, they retreated into offices and cars – a modern rendition of the old-time siesta – and the tourists came out in droves.

He watched a family file into a sweet shop. Canadian, he thought. Studied politeness and repetitious apologies gave away their nationality. They emerged twenty minutes later, tiny cups of melted chocolate balanced on fingertips, soft bread pastries thick with almonds and honey. Halfway down the block the same pedestrians disappeared into a French style bistro and his attention settled back on the photography studio next door.

A moment later, Almeida emerged.

Savio remained on the street after the car had driven away.

Rumor claimed Almeida's elusive niece frequented the establishment. In the last two days he'd uncovered a sizable amount of detail about Aurelia, all of which indicated her uncle might intend to groom her for a role in the family business. A scenario he found troublesome. Savio wondered if Rodrigo felt threatened by the idea.

In addition to feeding the insatiable appetites of the tourists, the shops along this street catered to unusual preferences. Perhaps Almeida's visit was personal. Every vice had a price in today's world. You just had to know where to look and have the money to pay. Check and check. Mexico City was no different. His lazy posture and indifference branded him with a purpose. Inactivity was a hallmark, a tell to be avoided. Today there wasn't time for stealth. He needed action.

Soon Almeida would run out of patience.

In general, Savio made a practice not to indulge in introspection. He acted. He relied on motion, movement, and purpose. He never second-guessed, waffled, or prevaricated over his choices. Not knowing if his allies conspired against him fucked with his head, hard.

Maybe he suffered from arrested development. Somewhere his ability to connect with other people, to embrace the desire for human connection, had been stunted. Not in a sociopathic way – he'd trained to turn off his humanity. The switch that disconnected emotion from action was worn out, the toggle loosened from too much repetitive use.

*Shit.* Despite his efforts to subdue the impulse, he was about to introspect

He removed the pack of cigarillos from his pocket. His eyes never left the storefront. In the afternoon gloom, the sky darkened. Clouds refused to drop their load of moisture and lent an atmospheric quality similar to old horror movies. He stared at the backlit square of glass. Inside the shop two figures stood behind the counter. He bent his face down and peered through the aperture of the tiny scope he'd tucked in beside the little cigars. A blur of color and motion sharpened into focus and he caught the tableau in the viewer and made the identification.

It was Aurelia.

The girl appeared only minutes after her uncle's departure. Had Almeida known how to find her all along or did he act on the same conclusion he'd reached, treating this location as a potential point of contact? The files he'd inherited from the detective agency recorded her in proximity to the building on more than one occasion.

She remained the elusive factor.

Savio decided to approach her. He slipped the scope back in the pack of smokes. Shoving the cigarillos in his shirt pocket, he jerked into motion. Favoring his right leg, he stalked across the street and furrowed through a cluster of college-age co-eds hovering outside the next-door café. A tangle of Persian curses followed him as he pushed inside the photo studio. A bell jangled as the wooden and glass panel shut. He zeroed in on the occupants.

Aurelia stood beside the clerk, a woman old enough to call grandmother. The girl recognized him at once and had the temerity to grin, the wattage sparked even brighter when he scowled back. Her companion did not smile.

The old woman wore a malevolent expression and Savio disliked her on sight. He raised a hand, palm outward and greeted them in Spanish, in a hurry to issue an explanation and calm their concerns. In rapid speech he laid out two options – neither of which appealed to the women.

The elder shoved Aurelia's shoulder toward the rear door. The girl stumbled and tripped over her own feet. She caught her balance. Both hands pressed to her rounded belly in a protective gesture, she ran. The old woman raised one arm, a machete gripped in her brown hand. She shook the blade at him and a stream of invective poured from her mouth.

The window exploded behind Savio. Glass shards pelted his head.

A crowd rushed inside but pulled back when faced with the old harridan and her blade. She brandished the eighteen inch machete and shrieked out a curse.

Savio ignored the shouted threats as he dove after the girl. He ducked under the wooden counter and glanced over his shoulder. A chair hung by two legs in the empty window frame. He recognized several of the kids from the café scrambling against each other to retreat through the door. He darted around a corner and charged down the hall in pursuit of Aurelia. The whoop-whoop of sirens indicated police cars converging on the scene.

*Too fast for regular law enforcement.*

She'd made him and called the cops. Now a bigger trickier competition was afoot. The do-gooders better hope they escaped before the cavalry arrived. Good deeds didn't always work out for the best. More often than not you wound up in jail until somebody paid the cost of property damages. If you were lucky, you got a cot.

The hallway led to a single rear exit but instead of opening to an alley, the corridor merged into a central interior access along with a dozen other doors. The storefronts masked taller office buildings and this served as the service entrance.

He had no way to know which direction Aurelia had fled. The girl could hide ten feet from his present position or be the next block over. He guessed and sped to the next door. He cracked it an inch and a whiff of sweet air filled his nostrils as he entered the back of the candy store. The scent of chocolate and spice overwhelmed his senses. He was in the kitchen. With a brazen attitude he strode into the front of the shop where two young women worked behind the counter.

"Culinary inspection," he barked at the clerk.

Both jumped at the sound of his voice but neither appeared surprised by his emergence from the rear of the establishment. One girl had a mop of red hair, a color too bright to occur in nature. The fluffy mounds on top of her head reminded Savio of cinnamon taffy. A swift flick of her eyes deferred responsibility to the girl at the register.

Savio shifted his attention but the cashier shrugged.

"The clipboard by the door has the current license. Mr. Cruz makes sure he pays on time." She told him. She counted coins and handed change to a customer.

"I'll just check the store-front." Savio exited on to the street and a blast of voices came behind him. He resisted the urge to look back and moved along the sidewalk at an even pace. He kept his stride casual as he walked away from the scene of the altercation.

In a busy tourist area the large numbers of people present didn't necessarily mean a trap, especially not one directed at him. Not unless it had been laid by Eduardo Almeida. A disconcerting thought. Or, a third entity had entered the playing field. That thought didn't make him feel any better.

His personal philosophy required arduous adherence to rules. He exacted tough physical terms when faced with bad guys. Right now, he didn't know who was on which side. That made him cranky.

Every day the shit just got more complicated.

He was sure the crowd outside the cafe had been organized, like a military group of some color. They were too disciplined for college kids, but they lacked the precision and reaction time of trained forces. Rebels, he decided.

Aurelia was the pivot point. He needed to step up his search.

# CHAPTER SIX

THE MORNING QUIET, broken by the chatter of yard maintenance equipment from nearby estates, reminded Savio of the suburbs. Despite that, he inhaled a deep breath and enjoyed the scent of flower blooms from the vines below the balcony.

Yes, a coffee on the terrace might help dispel his boredom but so would the adrenalin rush of killing someone. And he had the urge to act. Fillone *was* dead. Last night Savio logged into a secure connection using the remote link on the computer inside his locked office and found the death certificate. The terse report, buried deep in the files, he'd located by searching the internal file system. He'd finally uncovered the proof on Marco Fillone with a cross-referenced random search of Spanish words. The documents were listed by street name. Someone had gone to the trouble of deliberately clouding the information. Sabotage. Savio didn't know if the data was moved to hamper his investigation or hide the details from other curious eyes.

At first he'd been chagrined by the realization that without Cole's phone call, he might not have considered Henri culpable. Not in a serious way. He trusted Henri, thought of him as an infallible source of information. They had history.

*Note the use of the past tense.*

Savio no longer toed the line. Not anymore. He'd been a by-the-book soldier, a hard worker, a steady reliable type, a drone bee. A lifer, until the bomb. The explosion tore apart his body and altered his future. Now, he was unpredictable. Months of pain and therapy followed reconstructive surgery. Endless rounds of counselors and their nosy questions, where he'd learned to tell the staff what they wanted to hear. He'd have said anything to ensure his release. Those times dimmed in his memory. Now, the rush mattered. Work provided opportunity. He might go down this time or the next. Didn't much matter, one day would mark his last. Everybody in the business acknowledged that truth.

His thoughts circled back around to the business at hand. So, what mattered to Henri? Henri claimed Fillone had departed Mexico City only recently. Almeida had been searching for the man for at least two months. The records he'd uncovered in the computer documented Fillone left the country more than four months ago. The photo showed the man had taken a bullet behind the ear, the sign of a professional hit. Certainly a cleaner swifter death than Almeida promised. Aurelia's pregnancy correlated the dates. Now that he'd seen her up close, she was obviously pregnant, easily far enough along that Fillone *could* have fathered the child. Savio didn't know what kind of transactions Fillone specialized in or with whom he'd conducted business. Regardless, a projectile could catch a victim unaware. Some never saw or heard one coming.

His job morphed, took on a new shape.

Savio had to decide who to trust, the man in charge or his old comrade-in-arms. Only one of them signed his paycheck. As a mercenary of sorts, he followed the money. That was easy.

The weather had turned warm. On the back balcony, Savio stood with a lit cigar in one hand and a cup of coffee in the other. He admired the sparkle of water in the pool, a bright jewel amid the greenery. In his youth he'd swam like a dolphin. He cut off the memory and stepped forward into the sun. The heat felt good after the cool night. He rolled his shoulders to loosen muscles stiff from the too-soft mattress. He pulled on the Cuban cigar, rolling the flavor through his mouth, enjoying the expensive blend before exhaling a cloud of smoke. Even Fillone's taste in cigars was superb. How could a man who demonstrated such taste be such a loser?

Slumped against the iron railing, Savio wedged a shoe under the edge and faced a harsh truth. Things were not what they seemed. Henri's agitation looked increasingly like guilt. Cole had been briefed with details of a mission different from the one he'd been sent out to accomplish. Power plays were in motion. He wished he knew which team's colors he wore. And on top of the drama, an odd thought took root, one he couldn't shake. He was bored by it all.

The view from the balcony was expansive. Above the trees he identified the dark heart of Mexico City but he found the sight depressing. In an attempt to prepare for the leap into the massive crush of downtown traffic, he gazed across the valley. Today, a thick layer of smog hung above the peaked rooflines of the colonial district. He didn't have to see the lines of vehicles snaking through the streets to know the exhaust fumes would choke the air. The drive to Almeida's office would take an hour plus, but it was confrontation time.

An elaborate effort painted his landlord as the seducer of little girls. Regardless if that was true, the man was dead. Savio suspected the baby Aurelia carried had been fathered by Fillone. The calendar matched. In the eyes of a teenage lover, Fillone might have appeared to take on the role of savior. Marriage to a wealthy powerful man offered a haven from Almeida's influence, or so Aurelia might have thought. Young girls were liable to be romantic about such things.

The company dossier on Eduardo Almeida indicated a man who dealt with competitors in a decisive manner. He used violence to make a point. Ruthless hands fashioned obedience at the same time discontent was bred. He would not be surprised to learn Fillone and Almeida had personal dealings. The men were acquainted. The killing of one could easily revolve around revenge. If not, then how did Aurelia fit into the picture? Perhaps Enrique's story of Aurelia being in cahoots with another family member held some truth after all.

Information had value. Whoever controlled the right details would be sought after by someone. It behooved Savio to be in just such a position.

The envelope he'd acquired from Almeida contained the results of the private inquiries investigators had made into Aurelia's whereabouts. The contents covered the table in front of him. He scattered the photos in an array so he could study her face from multiple angles. Several papers contained notes about surveillance details. He picked up those pages and flipped through them once more.

Aurelia's strong features and high cheekbones indicated indigenous ancestry. The street name of Palenque made sense to him. She bore the same profile as the carved reliefs found on the walls of the ancient city in southern Mexico. He'd perused pictures of the site on the internet, curious if Aurelia had taken the title for herself and wondering what importance the word held in her life. He appreciated the irony of Aurelia's uncanny resemblance to the King of Copán. They shared the long nose, high forehead, and well-shaped lips – enough to make him think she might be a descendent. He studied the inverted photographs, searching for identifying marks. Anything memorable enough to stand out in a crowd escaped him.

The girl had a dark complexion and straight black hair. He thought about this observation. Almeida and his sister were light-skinned, their heritage drawn from blended origins. The girl must favor her father in looks.

Aurelia's large eyes sat a trifle close together. They dominated her narrow face. Not beautiful in the classic sense but the lens captured a certain quality. Even in the photograph he sensed a spark of fiery spirit. One picture caught her hair brushed back by a hand, her fingernails painted a brilliant blue, the punch of color a vivid contrast to her dark coloring. The report stated a petite frame at five feet tall and a hundred pounds. He studied the vital statistics and his blood pressure erupted when he noted her birthdate. She'd turned fifteen the previous month.

He stubbed out the smoke and shoved his fingers through his hair. On his scalp, he traced two small raised scars, mementos of an explosion last year. By comparison to this debacle, he preferred the dangers of the jungle. The process was no easier but at least you knew who to target.      Children were absent from the scene.

The distribution end of the business, made more difficult by the presence of players like Aurelia and Enrique, confused him. Shooting minors was an event you didn't walk away from with your sanity entirely intact. Some acts could never be forgotten. Or forgiven. This undercover work offended his moral code. He much preferred to shoot bad guys.

His eyes returned to the array of images. In three of the photos she wore the same clothes. In one of the photos he thought he recognized the studio in the background. In two of the candid snapshots she stood in front of the window he'd last seen with a chair dangling half inside. Taken with a telephoto lens, the image had been cropped so little scenery showed. The third one zoomed in on an interior counter similar to the one he'd darted behind when the explosion shattered the front entrance.

Aurelia appeared unaware that she'd been observed and photographed. She didn't look pregnant in any of these pictures but Savio knew squat about baby bumps. She probably hadn't been showing then.

For argument sake, if Fillone was ruled out as the father, who filled that role? Almeida? Savio suppressed a shudder. Enrique? At least the boy was close to her in age. Someone else? Paternal identity might not even matter. Now he regretted Enrique's release. His captivity could have drawn Aurelia out. He'd gambled and let the boy go free on the hope his message would spur contact. It hadn't happened and now he was forced to explore new avenues.

"Fillone will arrive at noon today," he said aloud to the room. He repeated the words just to make certain any electronic ears received the message.

Complications were mounting. He needed to move fast, jar something or someone into motion. He picked up his phone and dialed. A voice answered on the third ring.

"Savio Mendes for Señor Almeida."

The clerk placed him on hold.

A short time later the line connected. "Buenos días, Señor Mendes. Do you have information for me?"

"I do. I would like to invite you to lunch." He favored a public setting. Their last meeting had taken place in Almeida's building, in his top floor office. The information he planned to deliver today was best issued away from armed muscle with twitchy fingers.

"That is agreeable." He suggested a location. "I will call and make the reservation for one o'clock."

Savio disconnected. Events were in motion. Like a landslide building up momentum, things continued to roll downhill. Today he would lunch with Eduardo Almeida, the head of a drug cartel, and maybe they'd try to kill each other.

The restaurant sat in the Federal District near the capital complex, the seat of power for the country. Savio wore one of Fillone's Armani suits he'd found in the closet. A form of up-scale armor, the clothes performed in a similar fashion. Curious stares were deflected and inquisitive looks turned to approval upon recognition of name and label. He strode through the restaurant with confident steps. The fit was imperfect, Fillone weighed more and stood taller, but his unhurried gait set the right tone. His body felt limber and his mind alert. He played this hand on instinct.

True to form, Almeida sat at the finest table with an expansive view of the valley. Mountains speared the sky in a dramatic backdrop. Savio appreciated the scenery, wished he had more time to explore the environs outside the city.

He settled into a chair across from Almeida and set in motion his next offensive play. "You have lied to me, Señor."

Almeida's face settled into a blank implacable mask. He rolled his hand for Savio to continue.

Behind his chair, Savio imagined an armed man with a high-powered rifle aimed through the plate glass wall. His scalp prickled as he pictured the sights locking on his skull. He'd known this meet would be risky and a trickle of adrenalin seeped into his central nervous system.

He produced a grim smile. "Fillone is dead."

Almeida went still for a fraction of a second but then he gave another curt motion to continue.

"You want an explanation? Someone shot him."

Fingers tapped the tablecloth. Almeida frowned. He tilted his head to one side. The silence escalated as he studied Savio.

Almeida was well-educated for a man born to poverty on the outskirts of the city. He'd learned enough social polish to rub shoulders with officials and politicians. His gruff charm worked on both female and male acquaintances, opening doors to bedrooms and boardrooms alike. His rise in the cartel syndicate had been volatile and unscripted. He'd authorized key personnel to provide information to law enforcement in Mexico and the United States. Thrilled prosecutors eliminated rival cartels, a convenience that allowed Almeida's operation to grow with exponential speed. Smart men used violence as a tool and Almeida was an intelligent man.

"How do you deduce this?"

Here was the pivotal moment. Either the man across from him accepted the truth of his statement or the future would get dicey. The narcotics trade, never a peaceful industry, had taken a vicious turn in recent years. Wars raged over control of lucrative smuggling routes. Family members were stolen away, violated and despoiled. Dismembered corpses, often those of innocent and unrelated civilians, got dumped in public areas. All violent actions intended to incite fear. The method worked. People lived in terror, for a while. Alas, the endorphins cannot be sustained. The populace finds fault with government leadership and lack of progress. Vigilante groups form. The balance of power shifts. Drug dealers turned to new and even more heinous ways to cow the public.

Savio did not want Almeida to start thinking of creative methods of torture so he jumped in with his play. "I believe Fillone was targeted."

The bald statement hung between them. He half expected to see the words coalesce in tangible form above the table.

"By whom?"

Muscles tensed, he sat quiescent in the chair, wrapped in an aura of calm. "When I find Aurelia, we will know the details."

Almeida stared at him without enmity, his gaze turned inward.

Savio figured he was busy sifting through hundreds of interactions as he tried to discern a pattern.

After a solid minute Almeida refocused and jerked his head as if to clear a congestion of thoughts. "I knew Fillone. We did business. In my distress over Aurelia's situation, I discounted the importance of his interactions with other family members." He raised one hand and swiped his face, the movement jerky. "When?"

"Six months ago."

In a display of unprecedented emotion Almeida laid both hands palm down on the table top and fixed a piercing stare at him. "Show me the body."

"I will provide documentation." Savio folded his hands together and leaned forward, hesitating another second. "Fillone may not have fathered Aurelia's child."

Almeida looked stunned. His face paled, then turned ashen. "Are you suggesting they lied?"

Savio pushed. "Who would most stand to profit by the removal of both Fillone and Aurelia?"

"Not my sister! She is the one who told me." He stopped to calm himself, to lower his voice. "Aurelia confessed that monster had touched her. He is to blame."

Savio stared him in the eye as he spoke. "Perhaps, but the accused cannot defend his name, can he?"

Almeida's scowl became introspective. "No discord existed between mother and daughter until Fillone's involvement."

In that case, Savio puzzled over why Aurelia continued to hide from her mother. There must be an orchestrated purpose to all these machinations. Simple reasons Almeida failed to grasp.

"Is it possible your sister blackmailed Fillone?" Savio didn't believe so but he intended to sow doubt.

Almeida smoothed his hands over his black hair. When he raised his face and looked at Savio the strain showed. "There has to be another explanation."

It wasn't a question but Savio treated the statement as one. "Error is always a possibility. I discourage rash action until I find evidence."

If he'd been on the other side of the table various scenarios would have run through his mind as he tried to make sense of what he'd just learned. Almeida was no fool. He'd follow the thread Savio planted and reach the obvious conclusion that his sister lied. He would superimpose his own greed for wealth and power over the sister's simpler motivations to escape.

Right answer. Wrong reason. Same end result.

"As the messenger, you place yourself at risk to suggest such a betrayal," Almeida paused to heave out a sigh, "but I thank you."

Savio gave a casual shrug. "We are professionals. Now I am caught in an awkward position."

"I will ask the necessary questions of my sister."

Savio guessed Almeida's action would be swift. "I caution you to have patience. There are undercurrents in this escapade yet unidentified."

Almeida conceded the point but his expression turned dangerous. "I will refrain from rash conclusions."

Savio didn't believe him.

The silence was not comfortable. Almeida sat absorbed, his thoughts unreadable behind the blank square of his face.

Savio leaned forward. "My focus remains on Aurelia. She will soon be located."

He held off mentioning Rodrigo. Too much all at once might make the man hesitate to believe everyone was against him. Ironically, it might be true.

Almeida did not respond verbally. He tensed. He continued to sit but his eyes studied the tines of the fork he held. "I am indebted. My temper gets the better of me. Sometimes I make poor decisions." He exhaled a deep sigh and set aside the utensil. "Let us order lunch before we discuss more." He motioned for a waiter and ordered wine.

*Cold bastard.*

Savio found this performance unexpected and unbelievable. "Not everyone is destined for greatness. Within a structure of power such as you have built, loyalties can become divided." He was never so thankful for all his childhood exposure to politics and public appearances, skills which now might keep him alive.

"True enough. I have tried to educate my siblings and their children in the motions of the modern world, yet they hearken back to the old ways. There is no place for such nonsense in the global economy of today. Without my efforts, they'd still be in a shack on a scrubby stretch of land, tenement farmers, in danger of starvation. Now they live in a fine house. I provide all for them."

Anger mounted in Almeida's voice again as he reacted to the currents of filial dissent Savio had planted. This was not a tantrum by a man with too much power and too little empathy, but an expression of hurt. He'd offered everything that mattered to him to those he considered less fortunate. His family rejected his wealth. His control. Him.

The waiter arrived to take their order.

After he departed, Savio jumped into the conversation. "I have no children of my own but I understand the desire to offer your extended family a better life." Might as well turn the screws and remind him how he'd been betrayed.

Almeida did not respond.

Savio understood the enticements of violence. Poverty was hard. He'd witnessed firsthand the deprivations that drove people to desperate acts, but he'd also seen the most empathy and generosity among those with the least to share. Tolerance and compassion often sprouted from the leanest of gardens.

Almeida compelled others to bend to his will.

He made an attempt to soothe. "Perhaps your sister's choices are in response to this change. Maybe she needs more time to adjust to this new world."

"I took Aurelia in after her father died, treated her like my own child. She is intelligent and driven. I thought she wanted success." He glowered, anger clear on his face. "I brought them to the city. I rescued them from a life in a filthy squalid shack. I gave them a future."

Almeida was surrounded by desperate people. Distrust and jealousy, abuse of power was standard in organizations built on fear and blood. Trust meant everything. Retribution was harsh when trust was broken.

A new layer of drama, good thing he enjoyed theater. As

Almeida's newest confidant, Savio had been welcomed into the very inner circle of the cartel. He hoped to scurry out of town before someone questioned his participation in the family dissolution. Someone from the rank-and-file might want to improve his loyalty and put a hunk of lead in the back of Savio's skull.

Conversation waned as a stream of staff brought drinks and the first course.

Savio excused himself to use the facilities. Interaction with a well-spoken monster affected his equilibrium. When he looked in the mirror, the man who stared back was only half familiar, like an old friend once known but unseen for many years. A stranger you trusted and felt safe around even though all your instincts bristled with alarm.

When he returned to the table, he drank coffee and chatted about international news. In the darkest reaches of his psyche, Savio worried that Almeida wasn't the only monster in the room.

# CHAPTER SEVEN

**W**HEN IT FINALLY came, the phone call surprised him. The girl identified herself by her street name and in the seconds that followed, he tried on and rejected several different ideas for how to respond before settling on the role of intermediary.

"I hoped you would make contact, Aurelia. Thank you for calling." He paused long enough to offer her an opening if she wanted to speak. The silence from the other end of the line indicated she didn't. "I am prepared to reunite you with your family."

The soft bitter sound of Aurelia's laughter made him wince.

"What a liar you are. Enrique said you were a man with principles. I should know better than to trust his judgement."

"Enrique is a foolish boy but he is not wrong." Savio made

an effort at tact. "Perhaps I spoke in error, but your mother is prepared to welcome you home."

This time her laughter carried a note of merriment but it rang false to his ears.

"Just who do you think sent me out on the streets to begin with, Mr. Mendes?"

Savio rubbed his forehead. The entire clan was poisoned. He dropped the charade and opted for a direct approach. "What can I do for you, Aurelia?"

There was a pause before she spoke again. "Help me, Señor, and I will help you."

He set his drink on the kitchen counter and mentally crafted his response before agreeing. Then he counted off five seconds to avoid appearing too eager. "Let's meet. Name the place."

Five minutes later he merged the Porsche into freeway traffic. Half an hour after that he prepared to step into the mouth of a dank alley. The location where Aurelia had agreed to talk had seen better days. The pavement was a broken mosaic of asphalt, chunks of road waiting to turn a carelessly placed foot. Refuse piled up along the sides of buildings stank of urine and rotted food. In the heat of summer the stench would turn intolerable, but today the odor reminded him of home. He missed the dirty disheveled streets of Los Angeles. Leaving his gun holstered, he selected the center of the lane for maximum exposure. He didn't want to frighten Aurelia by lurking in the shadows. Not now. He needed this opportunity.

A burst of semiautomatic gunfire echoed from a nearby block somewhere to the east. The sound created a momentary lull in the ambient noise. Savio shifted his gaze, expecting to see a refugee from violence emerge from one of the alleys that cut between the close-set buildings like sluice channels in an aqueduct. After a minute the sounds of the city returned, whatever minor tragedy played out beyond the concrete curtain already forgotten.

This was his chance to gain valuable information, possibly obtain powerful leverage.

Savio sought the weakest link to exploit. In this case that proved to be Aurelia's mother. Over lunch the suggestion his sister had betrayed him made Almeida angry. No doubt the man had called to demand an explanation as soon as he'd reached the privacy of his car. Savio hoped he'd called because if he'd gone directly to the sister's home and done physical harm, he'd be left with little leverage in his conversation with Aurelia. The girl's response to pressure had been expected. The desire to protect was one of the best motivators around.

Working back from the center of the vortex surrounding Almeida's interest in his niece, Savio had realized family relationships were at the center of this complex equation. Business matters got mixed into the play because he'd assumed that drugs were at the heart of the drama. He no longer thought so. The chain of supposition he followed began with Almeida's half-sister and went back months. Newly widowed, Almeida had forced her to relocate to a life she did not want, but when she realized Aurelia was at even greater risk, she acted. Her plan might have been borrowed from some telenovela, but it worked. Perhaps she felt remorse about her actions but her primary concern had been extricating her daughter from Almeida's influence and so she'd capitalized on Fillone's absence to make him the villain.

Halfway down the street he saw the girl because she wanted him to see her. A flash of movement near the rear entrance of a cheap tourist boutique caught his attention. The building nestled beside the gated access to one of the prehistoric ruins that squatted between the glass and metal towers. Alerted to her

presence, he watched when she thrust out an arm, her white
sleeve extending from a dark door well. She waved him forward.

His fingers itched for his gun but he went.

She was alone. "Enrique said you would help me."

*Indeed.*

His original intent had been to turn the girl over to her
mother. Since he'd botched that by offering mom up as a sacri-
fice to Almeida, a move he hoped would not backfire and get
the woman killed, he wanted to know Aurelia's plans. "Did he
now? And just where is Enrique?"

"Removing my mama from harm's reach." Behind her she
opened a door that led into a narrow hallway. The space was
empty. A chair sat against the far wall and an accumulation of
plastic trash bags spilled out of battered cans. He recognized
the room as another of the internal corridors linking the back
entrances of retail spaces.

He welcomed the minor rush of relief that at least she'd had
the forethought to make an escape plan for her mother. He
hoped Enrique's efforts paid dividends. "Well done. I guess that
answers the question of who planted the listening devices at Fillone's."

She smirked at him, the likeness to her namesake again obvious. "Enrique was disappointed you discovered them so fast."

He'd hauled the boy through the interior of the house and
out to the parked car in the garage and all the while the little
shit had known someone would hear his yell for help. Savio
studied his companion and thought she looked tired. "Why bug
the house?"

"I kept expecting Fillone to return. Once he did, my plan
would collapse. You arrived instead and I thought we were safe
for a while longer."

So she didn't know about Fillone, or was faking it well. If

she didn't know he was dead that indicated someone else had killed the man.

Savio was getting the feeling he might need to get his hands dirty on this case. He'd done so in the past and understood the cost. Every price levied a mark on your soul. Nowadays he wondered how much of his humanity remained. Enough that he could let circumstances chisel away without consideration of the impact? Probably not. Every man had limits. But he already knew that if pushed beyond the point of normal elasticity, his conscience rebounded like a worn rubber band, snapping back. The tension might be less sure, the oval shape less perfect but nothing much would keep him awake at night. Only the ache in his bad leg disturbed his rest.

He plowed forward. "What is your immediate goal?"

"Why do you care?" She tossed her head and the movement rearranged her black braids. Her quick glance, checking his attention, indicated she wasn't as sure of her belligerent words as she wanted him to believe.

"My business is not your concern. What should matter to you is that I understand why you want out from under Almeida's thumb. There are other options," he flicked a finger at her belly, "for both of you."

Her fingers clenched into fists. With slow steps she backed up and sat down in the chair. "What options, Señor?"

He relaxed a notch. At least he had her full attention now. "Relocate. I can help you. Provide your child a chance to escape this                                        life."

She looked down, studied her fingers and picked at a nail tip. She didn't raise her face when she spoke. "The baby is Fillone's. I seduced him during my mother's birthday celebration. Later when I told him about my condition, he denied responsibility, called me a whore. I have no more use for him. He is a coward."

Savio digested this information. "Men are often a disappointment." The reverse was true as well.

She sat in silence. "I have my mother and Enrique." Her voice faded, her narrow shoulders folded in. Tired and scared, she looked defeated and much younger than her fifteen years. "I don't want this life."

The girl had attempted to carve out her own future. He respected that she'd rejected the role of pawn thrust on her by more powerful relatives.

"Your one real hope is to disappear." He could help. Being the good-guy was a nice change. "What will it take?"

She swiveled her head to look at him. Gone was the little girl, the immature gazelle with wide innocent eyes. In her place came a changeling, a woman of conviction. "I want free of them all. Let Rodrigo have Almeida Enterprises."

*Rodrigo.* Bonus confirmation he hadn't expected.

"If you help me achieve my objective, I will tell you everything I know." She offered.

What was wrong with young people these days? They always had an angle. He encouraged her to continue.

"I need travel money. A new start means we must have more than the funds my mother has hidden away over the last year."

"How much and when?"

"Tonight. My uncle will be enraged when he discovers we have escaped." She rose to her feet. "I should go. I'll ride the bus down the Paseo de la Reforma between eight and nine o'clock. Bring me five thousand dollars and I'll deliver my uncle's business dealings."

Five grand. Useful information would fetch a price worth ten times that amount. Whatever she'd learned was unlikely to put Almeida in prison but it might still have value.

He could afford the money. Cole considered bribes normal account expenditures. He had that much squirreled away in the villa but no desire to spend the travel time to retrieve the cash. It was a paltry sum. Five thousand dollars would fall far short of a new life for three people and an infant.

The thought gave him an idea. He checked his phone. "Text me your cross street at 8pm and I will meet you." There was enough time to collect the cash, if he could find an open bank. He backed out the door, hopeful this wouldn't be his last visit with Aurelia.

The game had changed again.

He typed a text as he retraced his path to the Porsche. Henri would complain about the lack of encryption even though he'd said nothing damning. After a brief hesitation, he sent the same message to Cole.

Savio's world was comprised of absolutes. He recognized shades of gray in the moral ambiguities spouted by the pundits on TV but he didn't subscribe to excuses. In his experience, you chose a direction, made a decision, and delivered on your promises. If you failed, then you demonstrated a lack of commitment to the job. The inability to follow-through on an assigned task indicated a weakness of character. He tried never to be weak but this job was leaving him confused about where his true loyalties should exist.

He paused beside the car and rolled up on the balls of his feet. Taut muscles stretched. With a minute degree of favor to his damaged leg, he held the position an extra thirty seconds. His physical weakness was another thing he despised.

Late afternoon closed around him. Cool air shuttered windows throughout the neighborhood. Although the calendar approached summer, an unseasonable chill kept all but the most unfortunate off the streets. In this part of town the itinerants had nowhere else to go.

His phone rang and he glanced at the screen. *Henri.*

Unlocking the door, he climbed into the driver's seat before he answered. He mashed the button and answered the phone as he veered away from the curb and into the stream of traffic. A line of banks edged the financial district ten blocks over. Almeida's operations were housed on the upper floors of a building several blocks beyond. If the clock worked out, he could tie up all these loose ends tonight.

He plugged in his ear bud and caught the stream of terse words as they came through the receiver. He waited until the guy ran out of complaints.

"We are not dealing with the remote coca plantations of the eighties, Henri. This is large-scale corporate business. The people in charge of this enterprise rely on their smarts not just muscle. Their operations are set up in a way that borders on legal. Deep fingers are plunged into the crevices of every level of government."

"So, tell me what you have learned. Is there anything new - something useful?"

He wanted to ask which operation the man meant since the one he'd been sent here to do had proved different than the one approved by Cole. Instead, he thought about the information he had tendered to the company. The data he'd sent in his reports had been useful intelligence but the critical details were reserved for his communications with Cole.

"I've learned that American representatives are negotiating contracts with Almeida. I got the impression these are businessmen from more than one distribution center, probably large cities, and the design is to set up a conduit stretching from the Mexican network into the United States. These smaller individual units take the raw components and increase the product in volume. The drug is cheap, the end-product is high grade, there's minimal risk in transport, and it's lucrative on both ends."

The method had been so successful that a surge of methamphetamine, unparalleled in the history of the drug trade, surged up the pipeline. The process hadn't been foolproof. A few shipments were lost, caught in border crossings or along the way. Newspaper and television reporters adored big drug busts. So did law enforcement agencies. Good press equaled popular votes and increased circulation. Major takedowns made the public believe headway progressed in the fight against illegal narcotics. It was a false but comforting scenario.

Henri started to speak again.

Savio cut him off. "This is a new way of doing business. The process surpasses the Medellín Cartel at its height. It's time to rethink how we deal with these guys. I'm telling you, this is a different world. People don't hesitate to import and export product because they're running legitimate businesses. Gone are the days when a bunch of street-savvy goons stomped on a kilo of cocaine to increase profit margins. Potential threats are referred to the police force and border personnel."

Henri appeared to chew on this information. "I need more details about the method of distribution. How does he get the product into the U.S.?"

Savio struggled to keep the frustration out of his voice. "The same way they always have, Henri. Planes and trains, shipping containers, tourists and refugees carry the majority of raw goods. Hell, they throw bales of marijuana stuffed with kilos of cocaine and methamphetamine across the border using catapults."

Henri remained silent.

Then there were also the legal routes of one businessman who sold materials to another. In the paper yesterday had been a tiny article announcing the death of an important anti-drug dignitary, a revered religious leader who lobbied in churches and on the street for reform. The brief mention had been located on the interior pages of the largest circulating news agency in Mexico. An indication of how little exposure the good guys were getting. Drugs were status quo business in the international community of commerce.

"Almeida Enterprises is a multinational corporation involved in trade. They offer an export product in high demand. If we're going to check this sort of industry, we have to find a better way of doing so, besides arresting the public players. The structures have to be dismantled. Even then, there's a good chance someone else will just take over. The old familial cartels schooled us in that truth more than three decades ago. All we're doing is squeezing off the trickle from one tiny stream while the rest of the rivers continue to feed into the ocean." Savio stopped speaking. His supervisor already had this information in his notes. In danger of being swallowed whole by the machinery of Almeida's interests, he expected the official word to withdraw.

"Keep on it." Henri ordered.

Savio closed his eyes and silently cursed. Already he danced around the point of no return. He was no spy. One day he'd be faced with a task he'd rather not complete and wind up dead.

"I'm already down the well, Henri."

"Failure means a loss of standing with the company."

Savio understood the implicit threat. If he failed to provide what Henri wanted, he jeopardized his future employment. Henri was after specifics. He'd made Cole think he'd gone out on a limb to back Savio in case his plan skewed sideways and he needed a scapegoat.

This might be the opportune time for Savio to demonstrate his history of going off the farm. "If I am discovered, Henri, I will die in a bad way."

"Then you have an incentive to not get found out." The words snapped out of Henri's mouth and echoed down the line.

Savio stiffened. Death did not frighten him, but still, one did not speak of a compatriot's demise in such a cavalier manner.

"You've worked hard to come back from your disability, don't blow this chance. We'll talk soon." Henri said and disconnected.

Cold fury swept through Savio. He choked on the anger boiling up from deep inside. Until today, he'd no idea how much resentment he held against Henri. The man had been long gone by the time Savio landed in the hospital. It angered him that he put into words what Savio most feared. He was not disabled.

He found the line of banks and pulled into the first parking slot, hurrying inside. His task required visits to two different institutions before he accomplished what he wanted. He returned to the car with the packet of cash and a plain manila envelope.

Behind the steering wheel he sat and thought. Why had Henri pushed his buttons? Time to find out. He jumped back into traffic and inched his way across town. When he neared the strip mall with the cafe he frequented, a black sedan pulled into the line of cars behind him. He parked in the lot and jogged to the coffee shop.

Savio's anger sparked the moment Henri stepped inside. There was no logical reason for the man's presence in Mexico City. He considered Henri a threat. That reaction stunned him. He shrugged off the emotion and carried his coffee to a table.

Henri joined him. His shoulders were thrust back in his banty rooster stance. Savio remembered the stiff posture from another life in another country.

"You're losing your edge, Savio."

The blunt words took him by surprise. He raised one eyebrow to indicate his query. He wanted to show amused condescension rather than the sting of truth because he *had* lost his edge. He knew it. He couldn't mark the date or time, but he felt dulled and torn, frayed at the fingertips like a worn pair of gloves.

Henri got to the point. "New intel exonerates Almeida Enterprises."

Had the man not heard their earlier conversation? He stared at Henri, unable to disguise the disbelief in his expression.

"Cole sent me the details himself." Henri said.

*Another lie.*

Despite the titles Henri held as old friend, former commanding officer, and superior in the company – Savio did not tolerate betrayal. Of all people, Henri should know that firsthand.

Savio stood and spun away from the table. He abandoned his untouched coffee and made for the door. The surprise on Henri's face satisfied him because the man had underestimated his convictions. Quick strides carried him outside. He'd backed the car out the space before Henri even cleared the entrance. From here out Savio was going underground. His task with Almeida was complete but there were still loose ends to tidy up. Then he would deal with Henri. Until the status of company security was confirmed, he wouldn't go home. Not to Fillone's. Not to Los Angeles.

# CHAPTER EIGHT

S AVIO WAITED IN the shadows for the bus. He'd turned thirty-five in March and couldn't recall the last time he'd taken public transit. The possibility that his issues with Henri and his place in life were somehow related to his PTSD embarrassed him in a vague way. He jumped when a sharp snap of sound came from a nearby street.

*Might have been a backfire.*

Rapid feet pounded on pavement.

*Gunshot.*

The sounds faded in the distance.

This was not the time to stick his nose in other people's problems. He had enough on his plate. He set out to determine who to trust and decided it was easier to distrust everyone. Then he couldn't be caught unawares.

Almeida controlled every aspect of his business, which included the members of his family involved in his various enterprises. He'd sent Rodrigo to acquire bona fides in America. The younger Almeida would return to Mexico with a prestigious education and numerous contacts among the heirs of the current leaders of American business and industry. He'd pulled Aurelia and her mother from their rural lifestyle and transported them into a world of wealth where they were uncomfortable. A legitimate businessman, he was regarded as an honest man in the local community. He was well-respected. His public persona appealed to the masses. Despite the ugly side of his history, bringing Almeida down would not be easy.

In his position at the curb, Savio checked his phone. He ignored the string of missed calls from Henri and three new messages. He concentrated on the scenery, gaze moving in a continuous pattern over the avenue.

Drugs were endemic in modern culture. The larger the town, the greater the problem. Product was transported by air and land, sent by the freight train load through tunnel systems up and down the Americas. Hell, he knew about people ballsy enough to mail narcotics via overnight postage like they were business documents. Almeida had constructed an actual production plant. His holdings churned out raw product by the ton. Trucks carried containers to transport ships and routed his goods to overseas locations, the return loads packed with additional chemical components to manufacture more. Insatiable demand drove the industry. Differences in perspective complicated combat approaches to the drug trade. The difference of opinion made inter-agency cooperation intractable. The official Mexican view focused on dismantling the powerful cartels one limb at a time. The prevention of drug trafficking was often left to U.S. functionaries lacking the resources and capability to do much more than slow the flow.

The bus rounded the corner and rumbled up the street toward him. He stepped out into the light so the driver would stop.

Just like Prohibition encouraged the transport of contraband alcohol into the U.S. from both the northern and southern borders, today's poison of choice circumvented legislation and restrictions. Those old routes had never shut down, even after the booze ban was repealed. The product simply changed.

Aboard the bus, he found Aurelia at once. She sat tucked into a window seat two-thirds of the way in the back. He'd purchased a card from the machine where he'd parked the Porsche, and now he swiped it across the electronic reader to pay his fare. He strode toward the rear, his approach too aggressive. His sense of urgency escalated as the hours on the clock inched forward. There wasn't much time to say what he needed to, so he barged ahead and crowded into the seat beside the girl.

Even the driver stared at him via the rear-view mirror, brown eyes locked on his, alert and wary.

Good instincts.

Savio ignored him and after a thirty second delay, the bus moved forward. He shifted his jacket and exposed the grip of the pistol in his shoulder rig. A sharp intake of breath beside him indicated the girl had seen both the gun and the thick stack of folded bills he pulled from his breast pocket. A quick check showed the driver was no longer interested in them.

"Take it." He thrust the wad of money at her. "It's five thousand, American, enough to get across the border on the Amarillo Express."

She hesitated no more than a second. Delicate brown fingers tipped with purple nail polish snatched the bills. The money disappeared into her sweater. Her legs were toned. The mini dress bulged in front, the fabric pulled up short where her rounded belly strained against the seams. The garment had not been designed to cradle a baby.

"Gracias." She said as the bus lurched into motion. "Which agency do you work for?"

He stiffened at the speculative note in her tone.

She traced a finger down his sleeve until he turned to face her. She snatched her hand back. Nervous now, her palm swirled over the bulge of her pregnancy. At that moment she looked like a fifteen year old runaway.

"I am the only friend you have tonight, Aurelia. Don't waste time asking useless questions."

Savio hoped everyone got to live with the decisions that brought them to this place and time. He assumed Almeida would put a price on anyone's head, even a relative, counted on it in fact. Loyalty was of paramount importance to people in this industry. He figured it was simply a matter of time before the man disposed of the relatives he'd rescued from the gutter. Almeida had already indicated how unappreciated he felt about the women receiving his generosity.

"My uncle will seek revenge if he learns you have assisted me."

"No doubt." He agreed. On more than one occasion he'd decided Almeida needed killing but since he wasn't in Mexico under the guise of assassin, he'd restrained his impulses, more's the pity.

She pulled the sweater tighter around her body. "I'm surprised by his tenacity."

So was he. "Tell me why he is so concerned with finding you."

She twisted her lips in an expression of regret. "Who knows, Señor? My mother says he desires to prove himself as a leader.

She says he is always unhappy – with his life, his women, his family, and his business matters." She grinned at him. "My grandfather was a humble man, everyone says so. Before he died, he cursed my uncle's name and Mama says now he can never be content with his lot in life."

Savio nodded. In a way this made sense to him. Father figures represented everything their sons were not. In Almeida's case his father had been a poor farmer. That probably cut him to the quick. If the father found the son wanting, then being rejected by a sister was not liable to end well.

She shifted in the seat, repositioning her shoulder against the window. "My uncle flashes power the way a drunk man waves around money. People notice. Some of those individuals want what he has for themselves."

"Much like a drunk is rolled by someone more clever or sober." Savio finished.

She nodded. "My uncle Rodrigo is just such a man."

This caught his attention. He studied Aurelia, wanted to be certain he understood what she intimated.

She held out a hand and opened her fingers to display a small flash drive. "I agreed to send this to him in exchange for our freedom. He can't be trusted. He is smart and stupid at the same time. He goes to a fancy college but all he understands is money. He does not remember what it means to be poor."

The device on her palm could hold reams of data but Savio didn't reach for it. "What does it contain?"

"These are files. There might be something helpful to you. I don't want to know. Rodrigo thinks I haven't successfully accessed my uncle's computer yet. I wanted to pressure him into letting us go home but as long as either of them knows where to find us, they'd always have that hold over us."

Some advantages weren't easy to use. "You copied the contents of his computer?" Doubt crept into his voice.

She grinned at him and he saw another flash of her actual age. "Everyone dismisses the kid, right? No one pays us any attention. I copied all of Eduardo's document files. He must have information on there he doesn't want anyone to have or he wouldn't have password protection."

"How did you manage to get around that?"

She chortled, a gleeful burble of sound. "His passwords are always some variation of *mi abuelo's* name, Juan Carlos."

*Her grandfather.*

Lesson learned. He'd never again dismiss kids as incapable. Savio picked up the drive and tucked the device inside his shirt pocket. He buttoned the flap securely. "Thank you."

"You're welcome to it, Señor." She stroked her abdomen. "I just want a simple life."

He pulled out the manila envelope, curled into an oval from being smashed against his side, and handed it to her. "Keep my phone number. You never know what the future might hold. Consider this a going away present."

Aurelia frowned. "What's inside?"

"Fillone's offshore holdings. Fillone is dead. He has no further need of wealth he amassed. With no one to place a claim or make an official inquiry, the monies will gather dust until the bank collapses. At least this way, you have a chance. Since the child you carry is his immediate heir, consider it poetic justice. There's enough money to take you anywhere you need to go." And live in relative comfort for a long time if she kept a low profile.

The girl's eyes fluttered shut. When she opened them again he saw the glitter of unshed tears. "Gracias, Señor."

Savio exited at the next stop, uncomfortable with her admiration. The last he saw of Palenque, was her dark head leaned against the window.

The net drew tighter and the old cliché struck a chord in his chest. He stretched and tried to loosen the tension in his muscles. The constant expectation of violence just at the edge of his senses kept him keyed up. Nervous energy chipped at his patience until an uncanny premonition tickled the skin between his shoulder blades. The promise of a bullet through the back seemed palpable.

He caught sight of his reflection in the shiny surface of a window treated with sun-deterrent film and stretched, watching his image. The scene reminded him of a giant austere clock with the second hand clicking forward, one precise portion of measured time every second. He sucked in another deep breath, counted to three, and repeated. The inhalation exercise forced the strain back down through sheer dint of will.

He'd never been this on-edge. Sure, the situation was stressful. Deals with drug producers and distributors always held risk, but there was more to it than the obvious. Before Henri had slid the dossier across his desk, he'd sidled closer to the cliff edge. If he didn't soon exert some caution he'd free-fall into open airspace. The thought carried a certain dangerous attraction.

He wondered again what it would be like to die.

Did thoughts truly pass through the mind in that final fraction of a second? He'd seen men expire, watched the light and sentience fade from their gaze, leaving behind emptiness and a hollow sense of misery. Part of him yearned to explore that unknown vista, to know what the dead see at the end of life. The saner chunk of his psyche shut down that train of thought every time the engine tried to leave the station. Self-preservation overrode curiosity.

He shrugged to loosen the tension in his shoulders but the

ache persisted.

A car shifted gears hard. With a leap forward, a sedan swerved around a delivery truck. On the sidewalk, Savio flinched. His survival instinct was primal and with his nerves on high alert, he was jumpy. He began to walk. Right now he wanted to confirm Almeida's position. Though late in the evening, the man was probably still at the office. Working in different markets meant conducting business at unusual hours. Almeida was smart enough to monitor his operations personally. Savio turned a corner and headed in that direction because it was quicker to walk than to backtrack and retrieve Fillone's car. Besides, by now Henri could have tracked the GPS and be waiting for him. That confrontation he was unwilling to face tonight.

A motorcycle overtook a passenger vehicle and veered across the lane, headed toward him. Savio's hand dove inside his shirt. He'd half-drawn his gun before he realized the biker was no threat. The rider continued to weave in and out of traffic as he ignored safety rules.

He was definitely wound too tight. If he didn't find an exit from this situation soon, he'd shoot someone by accident. That would look bad in his report, but it might feel good.

The streets around him appeared empty. The assumption was false. Rain showers had driven everyone under cover. Clusters of pedestrians huddled in the shelter of overhangs attached to the entries of larger buildings. Every café and cantina, restaurant and lounge, boasted a cluster of dark suits. Arms sprouted from each knot, like a multi-armed human monster. Street traffic was light, a fact that set off alarm bells in his head. He turned down an alley and cut across several blocks, approaching Almeida's office complex from the south. Silent as a shadow, he watched the street. Water beaded on his forehead and trickled down his neck.

Something felt wrong.

Nothing moved. No single person or vehicle struck him as out of the ordinary, yet uneasy thoughts gnawed at his peace of mind. Amped up on suppressed adrenalin, he might imagine risk where there was none.

He walked toward the building and the night bombarded his senses with information. Motor oil and wet pavement tickled his nostrils. The scent of spices wafted from the Indian restaurant on the corner and roused his stomach. Sound was amplified in the narrow width of the street. Not quite an alley, the lane he crossed led to an underground garage beneath the office building. A limousine idled at the curb, but he strolled past, eyes intent on the main entrance.

A fresh wave of rain saturated the pavement, soaking his shoulders and the top of his head. A steady stream of cars drove past. The sound of their tires hissed on the concrete, their passage carrying new smells. He walked, face lowered and eyes alert. Somewhere out here were men who might want to kill him. He darted between cars, gauged the static-like sound of rubber tires on the wet concrete, and crossed the lanes. He disappeared into the alley, just another office worker on his way back from a late dinner, in too much of a hurry to circle the block.

The street turned dry. Moisture, unable to penetrate deep into the chasm, caught on the balconies above. Canvas awnings dotted with water droplets clung to the sides of the structures. The alley was narrow, so small a vehicle risked scraped fenders if they attempted to drive through. With a bit of a running start he could have leaped from the balcony of one side to the next. He considered the idea, calculated odds, evaluated the possibility of a fall on the hard surface below, and decided it was not worth the risk.

The urban landscape differed from the jungles he'd weaned his skills on. Nowadays the trees seemed taller and the ground harder. He was older now. The immortality of his twenties had faded along with the decades.

Many reasons slowed his progress down this path. He worked the job for money and the adrenalin rush. He celebrated danger. But really, why keep pushing?

He should shoot Almeida, just put a bullet through the man's cranium. Although his death wouldn't halt the metham-phetamine distribution funneling across the border. At best it would crimp the mechanism and divert the flow for a brief time. Results not worth the effort.

This might be a case of better the devil you know.

Savio sighed and the sound filled the alley. As often as he thought about killing Almeida, he resisted. Reason number one was stopping the movement of drugs. If he tracked the out-source lines and snipped off the arms, the octopus starved. Al-meida had built an empire using new solutions to old problems. Perhaps that was the way to combat his success.

Using a side entrance, he strolled inside the lobby of Al-meida's office complex and approached the bank of elevators. He selected the unit that sat alone, the one reserved for the top floor where the fat spider squatted in the center of his web. He pushed the arrow key for up and the door slid open.

Inside he pressed the privacy button so the car wouldn't stop on any other level. The penthouse level enjoyed a few perks. The climb lasted an inordinate amount of time, another anxiety symptom of his heightened senses. At last the car slowed and came to a halt, a little bump signaling the end of the ride. The door opened.

Savio spied Almeida through the plate glass windows of his

office where he sat behind his desk. They met gazes. The man smiled and waved him into the room. Savio stepped over the threshold but before his foot connected with the floor, the world blew apart.

# CHAPTER NINE

**L**IGHT FLASHED. AN explosion reverberated off the walls. The percussion echoed inside the elevator car. The bright aura took Savio back in memory to a scene where his mother danced on a darkened stage. She stood spotlighted, her slender figure bathed in a halo.

He'd been five years old. Perched on the upholstered seat, his feet dangled twelve inches from the floor. The outing, one of the many public appearances his father insisted were necessary to present the image of the modern nuclear family, had been a surprise. As a boy, he'd watched his mother dance every day in her home studio. He'd seen her pirouette and glide, but he'd never experienced this transformation.

In the cavern of the opera house the prima ballerina became the scent of flowers. She floated on the wind, swept along the crowns of the grass in the meadow, carried aloft like dandelion fluff. A creature of light and motion, she skimmed through air to alight on the tips of her toes as if all women could move with such grace.

He'd been entranced, swallowed up by the spectacle. Not until the single spotlight blinked out and the room was plunged into night did he remember this exquisite dance had been performed by his mother.

*His mother.*

Frozen in his seat, oblivious to anything but the tableau he'd just witnessed, he was slow to follow his father's motions and rise to his feet. Like a miniature version of the man in the formal dress clothes, he clapped his hands until the lights blinked on and displayed the vast expanse of gold and red velvet curtains. The stage emptied. The room which had been cold two hours before pulsed with heat and energy.

Savio's chest burned.

The man in the box seat beside theirs cleared his throat with an officious air and addressed Savio's father. His stern, unfriendly face turned ugly, his lips twisted as he pushed out a grudging admission of praise. He said the ballerina performance was fair enough.

Rage suffused Savio. Anger unlike any he had known fired through his veins. In his child's mind the man blasphemed this wondrous angelic creature who was also his mother. His throat shriveled too tight to squeeze out a fierce rejection of the man's mundane words. Instead he glared his outrage at the demon.

His father, ever the politician, and attuned to his son's response, had squeezed Savio's shoulder. He smiled his polite smile. With a nod of his head, he turned away in a decisive rejection. Such a minor act meant little to Savio. In later years, he understood the gesture cost nothing and damned the man's social status.

That was the first clear memory Savio retained of his parents. The beauty and emotion of his mother, the austere strength and power of his father. Norms he still sought to emulate, jaded and damaged though his efforts might appear. He'd come a long way down a very different road in the last thirty years.

Another boom shook the walls. The scene dissolved and he opened his eyes, just a crack at first.

Brilliant light.

The details of the memory disappeared like smoke dispersed in a breeze.

Realization came slow. There had been an explosion. Concrete and rebar burst from the rear wall. Bits of debris sprayed throughout the interior, tearing through flesh and bone, chunks of shrapnel imbedded in office furniture, ripping through plastered walls. Another rattle of gunfire produced a surge of panic and he fought his way toward complete consciousness.

A flash bang grenade blew his pupils. Stun grenades were non-lethal devices designed to explode and disorient human senses. Until now he'd never fully appreciated their value. The blinding flash of light temporarily blinded his vision but even now his pupils were beginning to respond. His ears rang from the charge, the disarray in the office space taking on a muffled surreal quality. The impairment to his senses didn't last long.

Within seconds the rest of his brain kicked in and he began to process facts.

His dulled senses heard sounds, shouts and yells, a broken off scream. He blinked his eyes until they began to focus. The pungent odor of chemicals burned his nostrils. His fingertips tingled as if his hands had fallen asleep. He remembered that sensation and questioned if they'd been blown off.

Fear spiked up his spine. Death was preferable to mutilation.

He pinched his fingers together. The sensitive pads on the tips of his index finger and thumb connected. He rapidly counted off digits and relief flushed through him with a debilitating weakness. The back of his head must have struck the interior of the elevator, slammed against the shiny walls.

He shifted. The experiment hurt. Pain bloomed in his skull. He couldn't focus his gaze to assess how much damage his impact had caused. Enough to shatter the mirrored backing? Apparently so, if the glitter of fragments on him and the floor were any indication. He'd sport some new injuries all right but no warm trickle of blood ran down his neck. Maybe the shattered mirror produced no lacerations.

Someone pushed at his calf. He jerked his leg but no hand wrapped around his ankle. Crumpled on the bottom of the elevator, the cold marble tile chilled his back where his shirt had been yanked up out of his jeans. Disoriented from the blowback, he shifted his arms and braced his elbows to rise.

His muscles went watery and limp. He inhaled and exhaled. Tried again, then another time. He concentrated. His lungs cleared. Instinct kicked in. He marked and identified sensory information.

A trio of pops registered. More gunfire from handguns.

The response was swift, the deadly spray of automatics.

The internal pressure in his ears released, his head recalibrating from the force of the blast. A cacophony of noise erupted and overwhelmed his senses. Screams and panicked cries answered the burst of bullets. Acrid smoke billowed through the door. The ventilation system funneled the greenish cloud across the interior of the fourteenth floor. Through blurred vision he saw the wall slide toward his lower body, realized the elevator door was trying to close again, and yanked his leg inside. Seconds passed before he realized none of the walls had collapsed.

At least the structure hadn't fallen down in a heap. Yet. The attack had come from the roof and the outside balcony. A clever move.

The sudden cessation of sound and smoke disoriented his senses. He tried to sit up, fell on one side, and scrabbled across the floor to the control panel. He jabbed the star button at the bottom, selected the level for the basement parking structure. The cubicle responded immediately and jerked into motion.

Gunfire pinged above him.

He practiced breathing.

When the car slowed for the next floor, Savio rolled over and slapped at the large brass half-sphere that locked the elevator into private mode. The mechanism caught and jerked and continued its descent. The two floors below Almeida's belonged to an import/export company also identified as part of his personal business interests. The building housed legitimate enterprises, part of the cartel's successful longevity plan. They blended in with authentic commercial endeavors. He assumed those levels were locked down in anticipation of the raid, any occupants left to their own devices.

As long as no one shut down the lift system or cut the power, he might reach the basement undetected. He bypassed each stop, continuing to drop in a smooth, if slow, descent.

Floor twelve.

He appreciated the privacy button, one perk of the wealthy he'd remember for future use. Out of ideas and hurting, he prayed for an easy exit strategy from the parking garage because his flag was flying at half-mast.

Floor eleven.

If he got out of this situation and still had a job, he'd have a serious discussion with somebody at the top level of the company about the way they processed clearances for intelligence.

The chemical odor of the blast tasted familiar, an echo of his military days. The trace of peppermint in the flash bang, followed by the sweep of automatic gunfire told him an orchestrated plot had taken Almeida down.

Floor ten.

This was not a raid perpetrated by a competitor but a well-planned strategic attack. The kind he had once conducted on behalf of the Brazilian government.

Floor nine.

A bout of nausea gripped him. He leaned over and gulped air until the urge to vomit passed.

Floor six.

Breathe in. Breathe out.

Floor five.

He puked. Every heave hurt. His ribs ached. There hadn't been much in his stomach but now his head pounded. When he finished, he wiped his mouth, careful of the slivers of mirror that adhered to his shirt sleeve.

Floor three.

He needed out of Mexico City. Whichever agency backed this mission considered him just another brown face in the headquarters of a drug lord. In the rush of the moment people shot first and made inquiries later. Dead stayed dead. Innocents became collateral damage.

Floor two.

Time to launch. The Heckler and Koch felt solid and familiar in his grip. His vision still unfocused and his ears aching, he relied on years of practice to guide his aim. The last sight he'd had of Almeida, the man had sprawled across his oversized mahogany desk, surrounded by papers and the torn pages of ledgers. His duo of bodyguards had been absent. Savio suspected that observation was insignificant.

He made it to his feet by the time the elevator slid past the first floor.

Almeida and he had competed in a machismo contest, an orchestrated dance of testosterone like two alley cats circling and sniffing each other's flanks. The shocked expression on the man's face had been genuine. Savio would bet money Almeida had been just as unaware of the danger too.

*Played.* They had both been played. Question was, by whom?

This mission had gone sideways from day one. The company hadn't done enough reconnaissance to provide substantial intelligence. Each interaction with Almeida peeled away a layer of Savio's anonymity. Instead of an observer, he'd become an active participant. He no longer trusted Henri. By default, Cole and his company were also suspect. He lacked a safe bolt hole. After this, doubling back to Fillone's car with the GPS tracking device would be out of the question. Too risky. He had the money in his pocket and the clothes he wore.

The elevator door opened. A wave of adrenalin engulfed his entire body. He slipped to one side in unconscious imitation of the graceful moves his mother had performed in his memory.

No one stood outside.

The concrete pad in front of the elevator sat empty. He saw no signs of the unusual event occurring 1,500 feet overhead. The banks of cars were silent, except for the white Buick backing out of a parking place.

Gun in hand, Savio sprinted for the passenger door. He jerked open the handle and slipped inside. Firearm steady in his grip, he directed the barrel at the driver.

The man hunched behind the wheel. His long limbs produced the disjointed effect often characteristic of men who were tall but too thin. He wore cotton slacks and a button down shirt, and still gave off the vibe of a country farmer who'd found his way to the city and tried to blend with the masses.

Savio motioned for him to continue reversing the car. "Thanks for the ride." The sight of the gun produced no panic. *Interesting.* On a hunch he spoke again. "I'm your ride-along on this delivery."

The man eyed him with dismay, more alarmed by his words than the bullet aimed at his gut. "Nobody rides along, Señor. It's a rule."

Savio waved him forward again, certain now that he'd stumbled on one of the couriers. Not such a surprise. They rolled through the office in a steady stream, receipts cashed out and new product issued. Mexico City kept a late schedule.

The driver of the white car took his appearance in stride. "We don't take anyone along. Raises more speculation, if you know what I mean."

Savio did indeed. "Consider this a training exercise. Your employer is exploring new methods of distribution."

The man's expression grew confused but he complied. The car began to reverse again.

Savio looked back at the elevator. The door had shut. "Where is our destination?"

The drivers glanced at him again. "Montana."

*Fuck me.*

Upon reflection, Savio decided this route back to the U.S. was as good as any. He'd never been to Montana. The trip might be a novelty. That assumed they could cross the border with only his California driver's license. Not so many years ago that would have been enough but in this day and age, multiple pieces of personal identification were a necessity.

Savio rested his hand on one thigh and continued to point the handgun at the driver. "There's some trouble upstairs. Right now you need to focus on getting us out of this garage."

The man swallowed. His Adam's apple bobbed up and down his scrawny neck. "The boss doesn't –"

"Consider it a given that Eduardo Almeida has approved my participation."

The courier's complexion paled and his hands gripped the steering wheel so hard his knuckles whitened. At last, he nodded and turned back to face the windshield, his eyes glued to the white painted arrows on the concrete floor.

They drove up the ramp, rounded a corner, climbed a second incline, and exited on the side street without difficulty. There were no flashes of light, no emergency vehicles, no armored trucks, and no buzz of helicopters.

Outside was uneventful.

Savio frowned. He tucked his hand inside his jacket and slipped the firearm into his shoulder holster with a practiced motion.

The driver's shoulders relaxed once the gun disappeared. Another hallmark of a man untrained in combat. Oblivious to the fact that body and hands could be as effective as weapons.

Many of the people he'd encountered in the drug trade were not hardened criminals. They were workers, simple men out to earn a paycheck. Laws didn't matter to them. Their concerns were more primary, a table set with food and essentials for their children. The truth was a conundrum to the rhetoric spouted by pundits and politicians. Drugs were big business. He knew firsthand that two sets of people made an income from the trade, the folks on the production and distribution end and those fighting to stop them. That was an uncomfortable truth. He didn't want to empathize with the enemy. Concern for the competition was dangerous to his personal health and that was another unpleasant realization.

Their progress continued unmolested. Successive waves of traffic never seemed to abate as they crept across town. The driver paid meticulous attention to vehicle laws. He obeyed every sign with scrupulous detail, the kind of behavior that often characterized novice drivers. He shifted on the turn signal and left multiple car lengths between his bumper and the motorist in front. These weren't signs of nervousness but rather the actions of a seasoned courier. A regular route into the United States meant stupid mistakes were not made.

Savio's lack of a passport would not be a deterrent, he surmised. If that proved incorrect, he'd be forced to resort to other measures. A full hour passed before he indicated the driver should pull into a gas station.

"What is your name?"

"Benito."

"We're going to go inside together and make some purchases. I'll pay for the gas. I don't want you to speak. For this part of our exercise, you are an observer. Understand?"

Benito nodded.

He accompanied Savio inside, calmly waiting by the door while he used the bathroom and washed his hands. They purchased an assortment of snacks and drinks, supplies to carry them through an extended journey. Keys secured in his pocket, Savio sent the man back outside to top off the gas tank. He stayed to follow the televised drama as it unfolded on the screen mounted near the ceiling.

The cashier showed little interest once they'd paid and engaged in a stream of conversation with the young woman restocking the candy aisle.

Savio watched avidly as Eduardo Almeida was escorted

from his own offices. Flanked by a full quadrant of muscular men in black combat gear, none of the figures wore insignia that could be identified but the caption along the bottom mentioned an international task force. That meant at least some of the people involved were Americans. No surprise they didn't admit active involvement. The Americans never admitted to manipulating the machinery of governments and politics anywhere outside of U.S. borders.

The raid was successful. The fallout would be immediate.

Who had sold out the cartel?

There hadn't been enough time elapse for Savio's information to produce trained professionals ready to storm the top level. The extraction team had done as intended. They blew apart the organization, wiped out who controlled the various branches of the distribution tree, took the figurehead into custody, and waltzed out with minimal press coverage. The news deluge occurred after the fact. The careful discreet photos of the men as they exited the building would be repeated in an endless loop for the next week.

Montana sounded even better. At the rate they drove, the border stretched almost two days away. Too long. If they navigated straight through in shifts, they could make Texas in twenty-four hours, maybe less.

Night driving in Mexico was not the same as Los Angeles. The *glorietas* of the city were crazy enough as drivers pulled into the circle from feeder streets and swelled the traffic stream like creeks emptying into a delta. Taking the defensive was smart as was knowing the language of local signage. The universal "you hit, you pay" edict applied in Mexico City but once a vehicle passed into the unlit and often lousy country lanes, nightfall brought a series of new challenges. He'd forgotten that only the toll-routes were fenced. On the back roads progress slowed in order to avoid the free-range livestock. The upside was very little traffic.

The potholes increased in size the farther north they drove.

"Do you think we should just drive cross-country?" Savio grabbed for the dash as the car surged out of another ditch.

Benito laughed.

They continued, the monotony broken by flashes from on-coming traffic. Bridges were narrow. Intersections were a problem. They slowed to look and listen before crossing. The first time the courier had done that Savio became suspicious.

"Why are you slowing?" He demanded.

Benito explained that not everyone used headlights. "So far out of town they do not worry so much about getting a citation. When the lamps burn out they must still drive to work, right?" His laughter sounded genuine.

Savio thought they were all lunatics.

The longer he kept Benito unaware of the cartel's collapse and Almeida's takedown, the better his chances of escaping the country. Although in this desolate landscape, no one would find him here. He needed time to sort out the details of recent events. He could hole up in a hotel once across the border, but he might as well take the opportunity to finalize this job. With his mission gone to hell, he needed something to hold him steady. Going back to the office without details about the events in Mexico City was unwise.

The journey dragged.

Six hours later the courier grew jumpy. His mellow demeanor turned to fidgeting until he finally blurted out a stream of pleas. "Please Señor, do not kill me. I am trustworthy. I never steal from Señor Almeida. He is good to me. I need this job."

Benito had pieced together a scenario, just the wrong one. He thought Savio was an enforcer sent to bleach the pool. Not an uncommon concern among lower level personnel. The men who performed the best often held short-term positions. In the drug world, it was the ultimate catch-22. Too much knowledge about an operation made you expendable. Guess the courier figured his time was up.

Nothing Savio said soothed the man so he decided to level with him. "Señor Almeida was attacked tonight. We are continuing his business commitments even while he works out his troubles. You've nothing to be concerned about, Benito."

The man's nervous panic subsided but he looked even more depressed.

Every village lined the road with speed bumps, murderous on the suspension of the aged sedan. The lack of electricity in the remotest locales caused them to hit the lumps at a rate of speed that left the car limping. Repeated scrapes across asphalt mounds had to be exacting a toll. For a while they lagged behind a truck and then a bus, eyes glued to the bobbing ass end of the vehicles as the miles crawled past and taillights dipped with the topography.

It was mesmerizing.

Savio was relieved once they entered an expanse of level deserted land. No lights lit the horizon. He hadn't spied a farm or town for more than an hour when the car began to slow and Benito turned.

Savio sat up, more alert. "Where are we?"

"This track leads to a small airstrip. We fly from there."

*Hallelujah.* He hoped the flight hadn't been cancelled.

They parked in the middle of nowhere. Benito shut off the engine and slouched in his seat, appearing to fall fast asleep in seconds. Savio experienced a moment of jealousy but it didn't take long for him to doze either. He woke to the buzz of a plane.

The Cessna landed in a cloud of dust. The pilot clambered out and hurried across to where they had parked. No words were exchanged. Benito and Savio removed themselves and the stranger took their car and drove away.

Benito climbed inside the cockpit, the backpack filled with ephedrine slung over one shoulder. This might have given Savio pause last night but after hundreds of miles driven, he took it in stride. The flight halved their travel time. Savio guessed the monetary value of their one piece of luggage had jumped from modest to ostentatious the minute they crossed over the imaginary geopolitical division, and even more so after the contents were cooked into methamphetamine. So much for customs.

They landed without incident, just another batch of deadly cargo slipped past the border patrol. The surreal experience didn't end there. On the U.S. side a dirty white sedan waited on another airstrip carved out of hard-packed desert pavement. The keys were in the ignition.

Savio slid behind the wheel. "You navigate and I'll drive for a while."

Benito nodded amiably. His earlier concerns seemed to have dissipated now that they had completed the worst part of the journey.

They drove away from the patch of scrubby salt brush. From the appearance of the locals they passed on the way to the interstate, Savio conjectured they'd landed on an Indian reservation. Once on the interstate, they turned north. Benito fiddled with the radio, occasionally picking up a Spanish language station when they skirted close enough to a populated area. They had pushed north into Colorado before news of the drug raid broke over the radio.

Then Benito leaped from the car.

# CHAPTER TEN

SAVIO JERKED THE sedan to the side of the road. He reversed until the vehicle came even with the man. Benito lay in a twisted heap, torso on the pavement, feet on the dirt shoulder. His head bent at an unnatural angle to his shoulders. Broken neck.

"Goddamn, Benito."

A sense of responsibility filled Savio. Was he such a monster a man leaped to his death before questioning his intent? Apparently so.

He put the gearshift in park and got out to walk around and look at the body. *Stupid idiot.* He'd have to do something with the corpse. He bundled Benito's body into the trunk for lack of any other plan. Under the circumstances he couldn't contact authorities. He could have passed Benito off as a hitchhiker, but he had no good explanation for his own presence. No luggage and no destination made him suspicious. And he didn't want to alert anyone at the company of his location. Technology ensured that would happen if his identification was processed. Knowing about Benito's family kept him from rolling his body into a ditch. For now he would have to drive around with him until he found a proper place for disposal.

He emptied the man's pockets. Identification, a couple scraps of paper, and a handful of receipts filled the battered leather wallet. The wad of cash, payment for his last delivery, Savio tucked in his own pocket.

Back in the driver's seat he resumed driving, taking extra care to obey traffic laws.

*What now?*

The backpack sat on the rear floorboard. He still had the drugs and he knew the basic process. The two scraps of paper he'd found on Benito each had a word and a series of numbers written on them. One said Concord and the other Riverside. The names of towns? Perhaps he would assume the courier's place and play the charade through to the end. He had time to kill.

Savio pulled out the disposable phone and checked the minutes remaining. The device was almost done for. He needed to purchase another burner phone soon because using his satellite phone would allow any interested party to identify his location. Thanks to the wonders of modern technology and the improved accuracy of GPS, staying off the grid was more complicated these days. He entered the first town and pressed search. Of the top three possible locations, one was in Utah, another in Texas, and the last one in Colorado. He hit paydirt with the town of Riverside—it was in Montana.

He'd considered every angle to make sense out of his situation, to explain why Henri had been dishonest and why Cole had been motivated to intervene. He still had no answers. Doubt grew as he drove. Henri or Cole, maybe both, might have engineered the entire debacle. He'd sensed something off-kilter, had smelled the shift in the air last night when he'd gone to confront Almeida.

Nobody knew his identity. He'd never been notorious. His was just one more nameless Hispanic face tied to the drug trade. Despite Eduardo Almeida's interest in him, Savio was becoming convinced that someone at the company had created this situation.

That rankled.

Savio was good at what he did. His job involved the primary acquisition of information. He specialized in intelligence. Part of his strength was avoiding attention. The company had many combat-trained field-operatives with military background. Nothing unusual there. Strengths were assessed and tasks assigned for his particular profile. Most of the time, he chatted people up while he drank coffee, smoked Cohibas if he was trying to impress someone, and observed targets. The primary difference between him and the rest of his colleagues was that he'd known Henri in a different setting. He set that aside for later dissection. If somebody wanted Savio dead, they had tried hard to make him appear lost in action. Why bother when a single gunshot to the head was quick? With his lifestyle, the end result would be easily explained. His decision to continue on to Montana provided time to figure out a course of action. Besides, his feet hurt. Every muscle in his body ached with inactivity. His eyes burned. No matter how much water he guzzled, the scratchy sensation in his throat didn't abate. Hunger and fatigue consumed him.

A sign caught his eye, next rest stop sixteen miles. He almost cheered. He had to pull in and rest. Sleep had become a necessity. In the last twenty-seven hours he'd barely eaten or slept. His eyes were starting to see shadows that weren't there, figures darting out from the side of the road only to disappear when he focused on them. His attention wandered.

He distracted himself by imagining the silken waters of the pool at Fillone's villa, fantasized about the warm fluid caressing his dry skin. Dirt crusted his fingernails. Sweat rivulets furrowed down his back, leaving sticky trails of perspiration and anxiety. Lips twisted, he found amusement in his desire to be clean. His intensity rivaled the way some men welcomed the heat of a woman's body.

The exit arrived. He pulled into the space at the farthest end and stretched out on the seat. Left knee bent with his foot on the floor and the right one wedged between the window and headrest, he groaned with pleasure. Flat on his back was sublime. He slept for six hours. The sun had passed the zenith when he pulled back on the road. The car, locked tight under the noonday sun, had heated. The lack of winter in Montana surprised him and worried by what would be happening to Benito in the trunk, he drove on.

The landscape was monotonous, a continuous sameness stretching mile after mile. He shrugged off his melancholy and yawned. His jaw cracked with the stretch.

Yesterday had taxed his stamina. Today had not yet concluded and he could go right back to sleep if given the chance. A quick check of the date on his phone made him grimace. Sunday. He'd missed his third scheduled check-in last night. The alarm would have clanged. Information transfer was in process even as he sped closer to his destination.

He considered depositing Benito's body out here in the wilderness except the grassy plains probably weren't as desolate as they appeared. In a city, he expected a certain degree of anonymity. People looked away. In the countryside, folks were nosy. Locals were alert and watchful. Metropolitan areas provided ample opportunity to hide the dead, a small town less so. The wilderness was the worst with its endless expanse beneath an open sky.

A boundary had been crossed, one Savio hadn't been aware even existed and he refused to call Henri. Trusting his intuition, he finally read the transcripts of the messages left on his phone. All were the same terse set of instructions from Henri. *Call me. Don't be rash.* Savio snorted. He'd been prudent.

The patrol car sat tucked behind a knoll at a turn in the highway. Savio spotted the cop after he'd crested the little bump of a hill. By then all he could do was act brazen and keep going. You didn't have to be furtive to raise suspicions. Some law enforcement officers developed a keen ability to scent a potential arrest. A quick glance at the speedometer showed his speed hovered right at sixty-five, a safe rate in this land of no posted limits. He continued toward his destination with Benito's corpse in the trunk.

The patrol car pulled out behind him and Savio checked the impulse to stab the accelerator and race away. Instead, he maintained steady pressure on the foot pedal. Sweat beaded on his forehead. He concentrated on the road, his gaze checking the rearview mirror every few seconds. His vehicle had a Colorado license plate, not noteworthy in a region where most cars boasted an origin outside Montana.

The cruiser hadn't flashed lights and the driver didn't close the distance between them. The afternoon lengthened and maybe the cop's shift was about to end. Perhaps Savio was just tired and para- noid. All were possibilities.

He climbed another rise and popped up over the horizon. A com- pact car with California plates sat parked in the gravel between the highway and the fence line. In the slanted rays of sunlight, the paint gleamed, a rich bronze hue. He caught a glimpse of a woman crouched beside a clump of grass ten feet from the vehicle. He flashed past, his attention locked back on the cop behind him. A ribbon of empty as- phalt flowed behind his stolen sedan, the brown car receding in the distance. Then the cruiser crested the hill and appeared to remain suspended for a moment. The official car slowed and pulled to the shoulder.

Savio exhaled a sharp sigh of relief.

Thank God for tourists from the Golden State. The owner had distracted the policeman from what could have turned into a delicate situation. He might weasel out of the stolen car charge but the pres- ence of the dead body in the trunk presented another problem alto- gether. Finding a place to deposit Benito took on new urgency.

The GPS on his phone beeped for the next exit. Benito was a pri- ority, but first, he'd make a quick stop at the post office just in case he got caught in the middle of body removal. Benito's next of kin might be notified once his body was found but a package containing the man's wallet would inform the family something had gone badly awry. Their worst fears might be confirmed but if his body never found its way home, at least they'd know something had happened. The idea relieved a fraction of Savio's guilt.

And the discovery of Benito should distract local law enforcement. *Bonus.*

After Benito he'd make contact with the cartel drug distribution connection. Food and rest came in last on his agenda.

There was a sign for Yellowstone National Park at his exit. He veered off and steered through a long sweeping curve. Next he took the left branch and aimed for the township of Riverside. He wanted to avoid the park. Bodies found on federal land complicated matters. Too much oversight from upper level management made law enforcement personnel take everything like a personal challenge. Local cops, less experienced and controlling fewer resources, offered a better choice. They didn't have to worry about the public catching wind and tourism dropping as a result. He slowed the vehicle and considered which part of town featured the most private dump site.

Guilt, he decided, topped the list of motivations. If he killed a man in self-defense he felt justified in leaving the body where it fell. He should have left Benito at the edge of the road, just another casualty of the American freeway system. The man's nervous hands and sorrowful eyes, the knowledge his family would mourn him, haunted Savio. The conscience he'd questioned if he still possessed roared to life. Did that make him less of a monster than Eduardo Almeida or only a killer of a different kind?

This question he didn't try to answer.

In the post office, he slipped Benito's wallet into a padded envelope and added the folded stack of $100 bills. The flap sealed, he tucked the package in a Tyvek mailer and filled out the label with the address on Benito's license. In the language of loss, the message was unmistakable. He mailed the parcel boxed inside yet another red, white, and blue container. Customs would cause a delay but at least he'd done his best to deliver the wallet.

Back in the car, the courier's phone buzzed. Savio studied the number, his memorization of the digits automatic. He might as well take the plunge. He depressed a button with the pad of his index finger and said hello.

"I expected you this morning."

*Rude.* Already he disliked this man. "Travel between Mexico and the United States is subject to delay, Señor." Savio pulled out his personal phone and typed on the screen. Most likely a pointless exercise but some criminals were less clever than others. "I have your order. Do you have my product?"

Static crackled on the line.

"I need the raw material to complete the desired amount."

So, this was the cooker. He'd enjoy this takedown. "Where do you want to meet?" Savio asked.

"Where's Benny?"

*Benny?*

"Benito is dead." He issued the bald statement without inflection. "A vehicular accident. My condolences. Was he a friend?"

The man at the other end went silent.

Savio calculated. The man was probably weighing the odds, trying to assess his legitimacy. He unfolded the scrap of paper he'd taken from Benito. The Spanish words were scrawled, almost illegible. Penmanship had not been the courier's strong point. He deciphered the numbers and rattled off the sequence.

The tension expired.

They met in a dirt lot on the outskirts of the park boundary. When Mackenzie climbed out of his oversized truck, the dislike Savio felt over the phone was reciprocated in person. An instant and mutual dissonance erupted between the two men. Mackenzie stood six inches taller and outweighed him by fifty pounds. Dressed in the wilderness uniform of t-shirt and jeans, his square-jawed profile was reminiscent of a Hollywood leading man. The guy's smirk angered Savio. He looked forward to wiping that smug expression clean. The dismissive attitude Mackenzie offered in response to Savio's questions also rankled. Nevertheless, they would conduct business because each wanted what the other offered.

Savio leaned back on the fender of his vehicle and studied his new adversary. "You understand that I cannot allow you to leave with the compound. It is a matter of trust, after all."

Mackenzie didn't respond well. "Benito trusted me. You should too. I don't let anyone into my production area."

"I must insist, Señor." Savio smiled, amused by the uncertain look on Mackenzie's face. Big men always underestimated a man of his size. They relied on bulk and brawn to back up their intimidation. Savio had long ago learned that outside of guilt, fear was a great motivator. One did not have to be over-endowed with musculature in order to strike discord.

"Making that much product takes several days."

"I am on vacation, Señor. I will enjoy the sights, relax a little, and observe the operation so I may convey your skills firsthand."

Mackenzie's face took on a sly look. "Almeida has difficulties of his own."

*He knew.*

Savio nodded. "Sí, this is true. You and I both know, as men accustomed to the nature of this business, the current situation is a temporary inconvenience. When Eduardo returns as the head of his family, you will not want to find yourself in the uncomfortable position of owing him anything." A mild expression of reproach smoothed across his features. He dropped his tone a notch, "most inadvisable." He was tempted to add a tsk, tsk for good measure but restrained the impulse.

A tic twitched in the man's cheek when he'd used Almeida's first name. Good, let Mackenzie wonder just who he was dealing with. He waited while the guy mulled over options. In the next few days Savio would contact the company, ask some questions, and evaluate the answers he received. He might walk away from this life altogether.

That unexpected idea brought him up short.

All he'd wanted out of the last year was the next rush, the next job. Had something changed?

He checked on Mackenzie. The man fumed.

The meth cooker was determined to keep Savio away from his production site. Understandable enough. Didn't matter though, he'd have his way. After three days of frantic movement, Dave Mackenzie was shaping up as the perfect candidate for him to relieve some aggression on.

He'd pulled up some detailed news data about the collapse of the Cartel on the radio. Almeida looked to be facing detainment for an indefinite period of time. Whether or not he ever saw the inside of a courtroom or a jail was irrelevant, he'd been removed from circulation.

Savio studied Mackenzie with open interest.

Could he just pull his gun, fire a bullet through the man's head and walk away? No. Okay, to be honest, yes. Without a backward glance and no sleep lost. Mackenzie made life a misery for countless others. But since Savio had not yet embraced the homicidal executioner stage in his current funk, he'd postpone a decision. Maybe do it tomorrow. If nothing else filled his schedule.

Mackenzie's phone rang. He answered and carried on a brief conversation.

Admiring the evergreen spires where they marched up and down the profiles of the Grand Teton mountains, Savio's attention turned to the skyline. He listened to Mackenzie talk.

Compatriots meant complications. More threads to snip, tie off, and remove.

Time for reconnaissance tonight.

His stomach grumbled. He badly wanted a shower, some uninterrupted sleep, and a large juicy steak.

The Almeida operation had encountered a hiccup. The organization would rebuild, reform, and re-establish pipelines. They only needed time. The evening news always moved on to bigger and better catastrophes before supply linkages reconnected.

Mackenzie ended his call and went back through the mine entrance, disappearing into the gloom.

Savio remained outside, thinking of the photograph he'd seen on the television at the gas station the previous night. He'd liked the image so much he'd searched the internet on his phone and saved a copy. Now he pulled out the phone and looked at it again. Amid the flash of cameras, Eduardo Almeida stumbled on unsteady feet, half-carried between two members of the extraction team. Disheveled clothing and a dirty face replaced the man's erudite sophistication.

It was the picture of a deposed despot and Savio savored the snapshot.

One wrinkle further confused the situation. Several different groups claimed credit for the Almeida takedown.

In his opinion none of the people clamoring for attention were capable of doing the job, not without outside help. The world of private military corporations was small. There were a handful of major players and this organized strike had been executed with professionalism. Savio suspected an internal Mexican security force operated through an external body of professionals.

Welcome to the brave new world of outsourcing.

At this point, he was so far off the reservation someone in the company should have pulled his electronic vouchers and tried to trace his movements. He'd been careful not to leave a trail but eventually he'd be forced to make contact.

Unless no one knew he'd gone missing.

They might think his body buried in the rubble of Almeida Enterprises. He liked the idea though it was remote. By now the dead would have been removed, the body toll counted and reported.

In the end his insistence won out, Mackenzie caved and allowed him to visit the hidden production location, an old mine dug into the hard ground inside the park.

Standing outside among the pine trees he breathed deep and filled his lungs with clean air. His phone vibrated. Turning his hand palm up, he looked at the lit up screen. Cole's name shone clearly against the blue background. The head of the company certainly carved a lot of time from his hectic schedule to call him up. Savio debated whether or not to answer. The company tracked all the satellite phones issued through official accounts but knowing his location in Montana wouldn't mean much. So long as his presence didn't invite a visit from Henri or someone else he no longer trusted, the company knowing his location shouldn't matter. After debating the pros and cons, he answered.

"Mendes?" Cole's voice vibrated with tension.

Curious to see what happened, Savio remained silent.

Cole said his name again and waited for a response. When none was forthcoming he exhaled loudly, the huff of air turning into a curse. "Look, there's a problem on our end. Be cautious who you trust. Watch your ass, Mendes." The line disconnected.

He'd been correct.

A snake *had* slithered inside the system. Coiled up somewhere in the dark, the serpent waited to strike. He'd have to deal with that problem at some point. For now, he'd follow Cole's advice and keep to himself for a while. Once his task in Montana was completed, he'd get right on that.

Savio slipped the phone back into his pocket and turned his focus to Mackenzie. Bouncing on his heels a few times to work out the kinks, a trickle of adrenalin electrified his extremities. He slipped one hand inside his unbuttoned shirt and checked his firearm. The Heckler and Koch slid smoothly in the holster, his hand molded to the grip. Right now he felt like releasing some steam and rattling Mackenzie's cage would improve his mood. He ducked inside the mouth of the mine.

# ABOUT THE AUTHOR

As an anthropologist, Lesann divides her time between academic interests and professional research focused primarily on the American west. Crossing genre lines, she pens both contemporary and historical mysteries, romantic suspense, and even a little horror.

For information about other books and upcoming releases, visit WWW.LESANNBERRY.COM